Introductio

Worldcon came to Scotland in August 2024, attracting thousands of science fiction aficionados from all over the planet to the city of Glasgow.

For five days the cavernous Scottish Event Campus was a hive of talks and readings, greetings and meetings, ideas and sharing, feeding our eager imaginations, dreaming of what this universe of ours can be. At times it felt as if we were all travellers on a huge generation ship charging at near light-speed towards a new beginning.

Shoreline of Infinity/ SF Caledonia had a base at Worldcon, a dealer table in one space vast enough to house an airship. We met many fellow travellers who were keen to learn about science fiction in Scotland and from Scotland. By chance, our dealer neighbours were the good folk from Locus Magazine.

A stroll through Scottish Science Fiction

Pippa Goldschmidt and I gave a talk on our new project *SF Caledonia* and Scottish writers of science fiction to a full room of folk who went away enthused about what is happening here. They learnt that John (*The Thirty Nine Steps*) Buchan wrote a short science fiction story called 'Space' and they enjoyed a reading from up-and-coming writer Callum McSorley. Callum is only one of several Scottish new young writers who had a chance this weekend to meet a new audience.

Pippa said in her talk:

"Why is Scotland such a good place to create SF? For centuries it's generated human thought that has enlarged our sense of time, space and life. James Hutton, the father of geology, argued that the Earth was millions of times older than the Biblical age, thus expanding our idea of time. The physics department at Glasgow University pioneered the detection of gravitational waves,

SF CALEDONIA

ANTHOLOGY ONE

A SHOWCASE OF SCOTTISH SCIENCE FICTION, FANTASY AND SPECULATIVE FICTION

EDITED BY
NOEL CHIDWICK

ISBN 978-1-7395359-3-3

Publisher
Shoreline of Infinity Publications / The New Curiosity Shop
Edinburgh, Scotland

www.shorelineofinfinity.com

SHORELINE
OF INFINITY

SF Caledonia

Founder, Editor:
Noel Chidwick

Contributing Editor
(Non-fiction):
Pippa Goldschmidt

Contributing Editor
(Speculative fiction):
Chris Kelso

Cover Art:
'Yes', by Stref

SF Caledonia
is a free online
magazine and
resource of short
stories, articles and
poetry written by
Scottish SF writers.
It's a space for
Scotland to show
off its talented
community of
science fiction/
speculative fiction/
fantasy writers to the
world – and beyond.

First contact
www.sfcaledonia.scot
contact@sfcaledonia.scot

Contents

SF Caledonia

Founder, Editor:
Noel Chidwick

Contributing Editor
(Non-fiction):
Pippa Goldschmidt

Contributing Editor
(Speculative fiction):
Chris Kelso

Cover Art:
'Yes', by Stref

SF Caledonia
is a free online
magazine and
resource of short
stories, articles and
poetry written by
Scottish SF writers.
It's a space for
Scotland to show
off its talented
community of
science fiction/
speculative fiction/
fantasy writers to the
world – and beyond.

First contact
www.sfcaledonia.scot
contact@sfcaledonia.scot

Contents

SF CALEDONIA ANTHOLOGY ONE

A SHOWCASE OF SCOTTISH SCIENCE FICTION, FANTASY AND SPECULATIVE FICTION

EDITED BY
NOEL CHIDWICK

ISBN 978-1-7395359-3-3

© 2025 *Shoreline of Infinity*
Contributors retain copyright of own work

Publisher
Shoreline of Infinity Publications /
The New Curiosity Shop
Edinburgh, Scotland

www.shorelineofinfinity.com

SHORELINE OF **INFINITY**

invisible radiation propagating through the Universe. Dolly the sheep, born at the Roslin Institute, was the first mammal to be cloned from adult cells, changing our ideas of how life can start.

"Every nation has its own origin story, but in Scotland – with our debates on how we want to govern ourselves – perhaps our own origin story is lying in the future. That's SF."

There were many events where Scots displayed their skills, none so much as the shoulder-to-shoulder standing room only launch of the anthology of new stories by Scottish writers, *Nova Scotia Volume 2*, edited by Neil Williamson and Andrew J. Wilson, and published by Luna Press. The launch was a celebration of the Scottish SF community, with so many writers in the audience cheering for their colleagues.

In the ten years I have been working on Shoreline of Infinity and SF Caledonia, it has been a privilege to be part of such a community, a communuty whose members congratulate a writer's new book deal or encourage a novice to complete their first short story with equal enthusiasm. Out of that sense of togetherness sprouted Cymera, Scotland's annual Festival of Science Fiction, Fantasy & Horror Writing, now in its seventh year.

At our Worldcon table we were happy to help our back catalogue of Shoreline of Infinity magazines be crammed into bags ready to fly out around the world. Many issues, we're proud to say, included first-time published stories from these youthful Scottish voices, diverse and energetic.

Worldcon Glasgow 2024 reinforced what we knew all along, but perhaps haven't appreciated fully – Scotland is acknowledged around the world as a place of imagination, innovation and inspiration.

Which brings us to what you hold in your hands - *SF Caledonia Anthology One*. On the web, SF Caledonia has infinite capacity. In print we can provide a snapshot, an impression. So, sit back in your own capsule of comfort to enjoy what, we plan, is only the first of a long series.

Noel Chidwick
Founder, Editor, SF Caledonia
Co-founder, Editor-in-Chief, Shoreline of Infinity

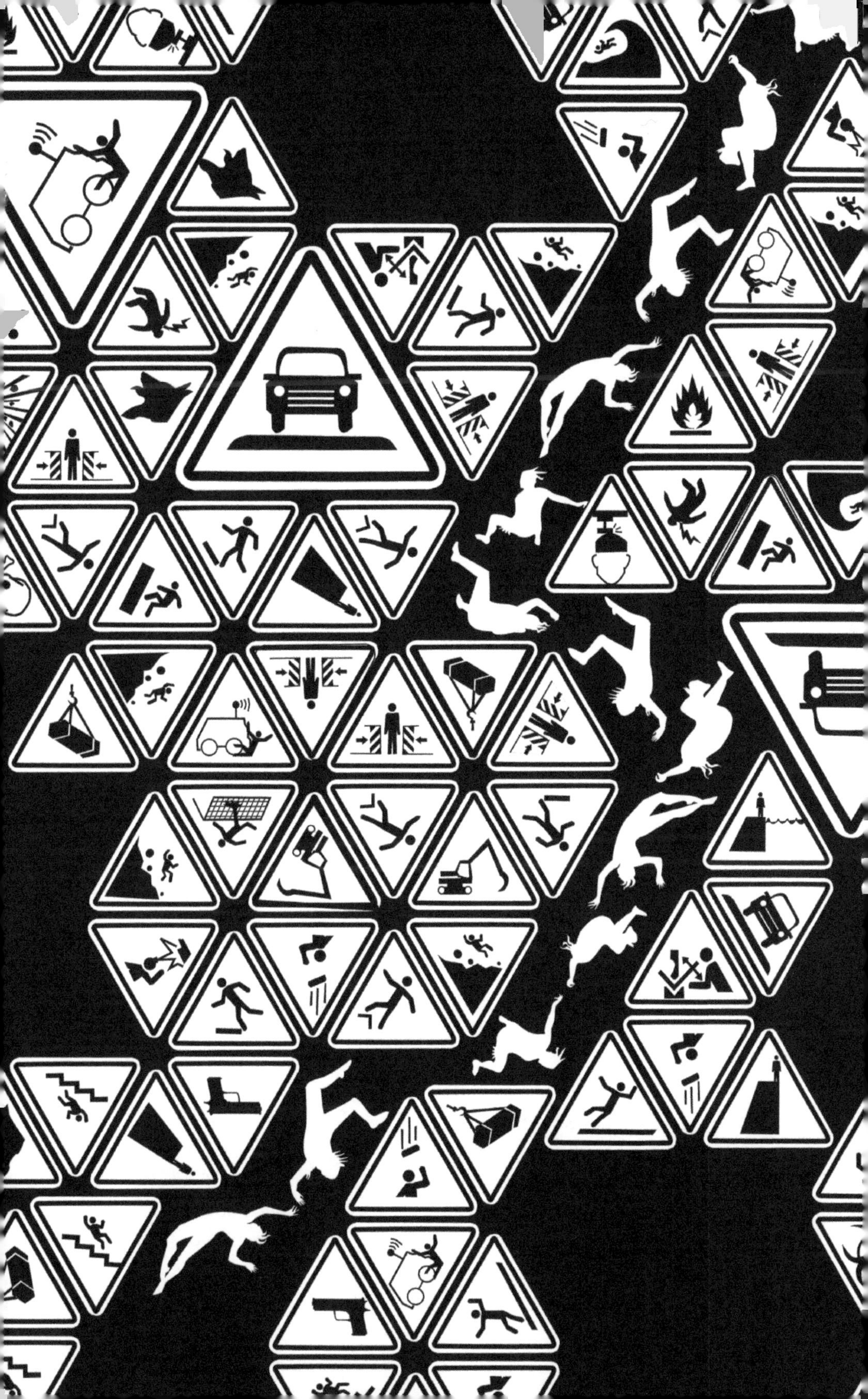

The Anxiety Gene

Rhiannon A Grist

I stumble back onto the pavement, but five other me's don't. Three roll across the hood, skulls smashed open on the windshield, the boot or the road still smoking with tyre-burn behind. One me gets caught by the front bumper and pulled under the wheels. The last is dragged a good few yards before the car finally comes to a stop, leaving a pink pencil eraser mark along the tarmac. I witness every terrifying sensation first-hand, from the smell of burnt rubber to the toe-squelch of blood pooling in my boots.

But I'm fine. The me that's here, standing on the pavement, is fine. At least that's what the driver in my reality sees. He flips me off and keeps on driving, completely oblivious to the five other him's and the five other me's he – they – just mowed down. It's hard to keep track of what belongs to my reality and what belongs to another, like getting mad at someone for something they did in a dream. But you figure it out. And what you can't figure out you medicate.

My hands are shaking so hard I barely manage to fish the blockers out of my bag. Dying five times over will do that to you. I unscrew the cap on the third try only to spill thick yellow liquid all over my jumper. Shit. No time to worry about that. I take a gulp. I hated the banana flavour at first, but now I love it. As the first mouthful slips down my gullet my heart rate slows and the fear sinks under a wave of medicated calm. I'll feel sick later but it's worth it for the relief. I shake the bottle and the last drop rolls about on the bottom. It was supposed to last me until the end of the week. Now it's decorating my sweater. I'll pick up some more tomorrow, but for now I'll have to make do.

Today's going to be shit.

"Congratulations!" The doctor said, "You have the Anxiety Gene!"

It was five days after my twenty-sixth birthday. I'd been dragged to my GP after my flatmate found me barricaded in my bedroom, a fortnight's worth of piss stored haphazardly in plastic take-away boxes under my bed. I'd been haunted by glimpses of death every day of my adult life. As I got older, they got worse. By the time my flatmate intervened I was unable to leave my bed for fear of some horrifying calamity and I'd eroded my ability to feel enthusiastic about anything, even a diagnosis.

"Count yourself lucky," he said, "We used to think it was all in your head. Now we know it's real. There's a testing window two weeks from now. Do you think you'll be free?"

I hadn't been able to hold down a job in years. Of course I was free.

I die once more on my way to work – ice on the roads – but my last gulp of blockers keeps the sensation dull and far away, like it's happening to someone else. My therapist taught me to see these alternate deaths like toy cars rushing through my mind. I'm to visualise picking them up, putting them back down, and then letting them drive away. I pick up the toy car girl on the slippery road and look at the world through her broken face. She still has a Wimpy's in her universe. Weird. Then I put her back down and she races away from me and I believe for a moment I can do this. I take a deep cold breath. I can survive a day.

I work on the first floor of a typical office building – all glass, stone and steel. Sharp, hard substances that could crack or bludgeon or cut. I avoid the wide glass staircase and head straight for the lift. I've had plenty of deaths in lifts – frayed wires, eager doors – but none on the glass stairs. Despite this, I avoid them like the plague. But today is obviously cursed, so the lifts are out. I sigh and head back to the stairs.

I hold onto the railing and take each step at a time, a nervous sweat beading the valley of my back. I can see our teenage receptionist looking at me quizzically through the glass walls of our office. I want to flash him a "fuck off" look, but I'm pretty sure the moment I take my eyes off the stairs something awful will happen. The glass will break and I'll fall to my death, or a splinter will fly up through my neck, or – and this one's the worst – I'll lose my footing, fall backwards and crack my head open on the cold glass edge of a stair below. But that'll only happen if I stop looking. As long as I'm looking at the stairs, they'll behave—

An arm hooks round my elbow.

"What have you done to yourself?"

Oh god. It's Fucking Linda.

Fucking Linda would be alright if she didn't feel the need to put herself at the centre of every story. If we're heading to the pub after work, Fucking Linda's got to turn it into an organised office outing. If our company wins an award, it has to be down to Fucking Linda's project management. And, if someone's trying to climb the stairs at their own pace, Fucking Linda's got to swoop in and save the day.

"What did you do?" She asks, "Go too hard at the gym?"

I haven't gone to a gym in years. Have you seen those running machines? Talk about a death trap.

"Thanks for the assist Linds," I grit my teeth, "But I think I've got this."

"It's ok," she says, "I don't mind."

She pulls me off balance and I trip up a stair. Not far, but enough to make me jump out of my skin. I push her off me and she knocks into one of the Support guys coming up behind us. He stumbles back, slamming his heavy backpack into the railing and spilling coffee all over his new-looking trainers.

"Christ, sorry…" Fuck. What's his name? I see him all the time but I can never remember his name. "… mate?"

He gives me this weird, hollow-eyed look, sighs and starts taking off his sodden shoes. Poor Support. They spend their days explaining basic computer functions to people who've probably never held a mouse before. Now this happens. There's only so much a person can take before they crack.

I don't know what to say so I scurry up the stairs instead, avoiding the kicked-dog look on Linda's face. She only wanted to help. It's not her fault I'm like this. But then again, it's not mine either.

The test facility was in an industrial estate just outside town. Big white building, still had that new sheen to it. I got dressed into a gown, wore bobbly wired hats and lay on whirring tables surrounded by an audience of excited doctors. Through some weird fluke of quantum-whatevers, the particles in the Anxiety Gene were entangled with particles from across the multiverse, forging brief connections between people and their alternate selves. The doctors explained that they'd seen this manifest as intrusive thoughts, visions, unshakeable feelings of dread or even elation, experiences they'd previously shrugged off as symptoms of psychosis, mania or – clue's in the name – anxiety disorders. However, in those flashes of connection, some people got glimpses of exciting worlds rich with possibility. I heard some could even have conversations with their other selves. A bloke I went to school with claimed he had this manifestation of the gene. Turned out to be bog-standard schizophrenia. Hard to tell these days.

I sat in the specialist's office hoping that the years of panic and fear would finally count for something. That I wasn't sick, I was special. The doctor pursed her lips and asked again what I experienced. Were there any other details? A glimpse here and there but mostly just the deaths, I replied. And that was that. Other people got the special kind of the gene. The kind triggered whenever they felt a surge of excitement – of discovery, of fear, of arousal. Mine was only triggered by the flood of adrenaline experienced at the point of death. When I'm eating a sandwich and some other me in another reality chokes, when I'm crossing the road and another me gets hit by a truck, when I'm taking a shower and some other me slips and cracks her skull, that's when my gene kicks in. I got the type where I die over and over. Just my bloody luck. I was given a prescription for blockers and sent on my merry way. I'm not sure who was more disappointed, me or the doctors.

By the time I'm ready for my mid-morning coffee the blockers are wearing off. An alternate me trips on a printer cable and breaks her neck on the edge of a desk. I catch myself from the extra-dimensional fall and scream. People around me stare.

Shit. Breathe in. Breathe out. Pick up your toy car death, look at it, put it back down, move on.

"Sorry folks," I say, cheerfully as possible, "Stray bullet." Caitlin in Web Dev gives me a polite chuckle. I wish people would laugh about it more. Ok, it's not very funny dying over and over, but it is pretty ridiculous and that's worth a laugh at least.

My Line Manager, Mac, stops me on my way to the kitchen, "Do you have a second?" Mac's chewing on a toothpick. Does he know what havoc a swallowed toothpick can ravage on the human body? Then again, he's the type to run down stairs two steps at a time with his shoe laces untied. I once caught him digging a bagel out of the toaster with a fork.

"Well?" he asks again.

I say yes before I've had time to think and we're on our way to a meeting room before I figure out what he wants to talk about. Shit. Of course it had to be today. I'm suddenly very aware of the uneasy feeling in my stomach and the bright yellow stain down my sweater.

It shouldn't come as much surprise to hear I work as a Quality Assurance Analyst. Turns out, experiencing your death in a variety of colourful ways gives one a prodigious eye for spotting things that could go wrong. You wouldn't think you could die from laughing. You also wouldn't think you could break a website by pressing the menu button sixteen times. Well, now you know better.

However, there is such a thing as too much care.

"I'm sorry," says Mac, flicking the toothpick from one corner of his mouth to the other. I smile and assure him I understand, but in my mind all I can hear is *I didn't get it I didn't get it I didn't get it*. I'm one of the oldest members of the QA team, and the only one who's still a Junior Analyst. I knew what had done me in. I'd been testing a new banking portal. After two expensive weeks of QA, I reported back that clicking the terms and conditions page ninety-four times made the font change colour. The dev team were fascinated. The client, not so much.

Mac follows me back to the kitchen. "Are you going to be alright?" he asks, "Just I know you can get a bit –" He holds his hands out and shakes them. My gut twists in on itself.

"There was an accident this morning," I fumble with the coffee pot to give me somewhere else to look. "I ran out of meds, but I should have more tomorrow."

Mac eyes my mug and frowns. "You know…" he says.

Oh god, not this again.

"… I read that cutting out caffeine might help. Less stimulants, better brain chemistry."

I try to mask the frustration curdling my face. "It's not really a chemical imbalance. It's genetic. The Anxiety Gene—"

He cuts me off with a wave of his hand. "Sure, however you want to think about it."

Of course he doesn't believe me. There are a fair few who don't. It's been just long enough since the discovery for the excitement to die down, but too early for it to really affect how the everyday world works. Unless you're a quantum physicist or a neural biologist, or me for that matter, the multiverse is just another unseeable untouchable thing, like Jupiter or the Higgs Boson. I'm not surprised people question its existence, but it's mind-boggling how many claim to understand my experiences better than I do. I silently place bets on which magical lifestyle cure Mac will suggest next. Vegetables? Or exercise? He looks like an exercise guy. He wears a leather bracelet though, so maybe mindfulness.

He tilts his head thoughtfully. "I know a guy who runs courses at the Community Centre, nothing too *wooky*. Just breathing, posture, help you become more aware of your own mind."

Before I can think *Bingo*, there's a bang.

Mac's mouth hangs open and a circle of red blooms on his t-shirt.

He's swallowed his toothpick, I think.

Another bang and the coffee pot explodes in my hand and Mac slumps to the ground. Somewhere in another probable now, two other me's fall with him. Now the screaming starts. There are more bangs and three other me's drop to the floor. I feel every shot like a punch to the gut. I can smell blood. Both here and elsewhere. I drop behind the counter and throw my arms over my head.

Oh shit. Oh shit.

Gunfire rings out across desks, shattering computer screens and light fixtures, sending sparks flying. Realities fracture in my mind.

Are we under attack? Is it terrorists?

I look up at the dangling remains of a strip light. It strikes me as a decidedly haphazard shot.

No. People don't shoot up offices here.

I remember the Support guy on the stairs. The look in his eyes. The heft of his backpack. Linda's coffee on his shoes.

Ok, maybe it could happen here.

While my mind races, twelve alternate me's give in to temptation and peek above the counter. All twelve immediately take a bullet to the eye, the forehead, the nose. Twelve! I've never had so many before. The multitude of deaths ricochet through my brain and my thoughts scatter like marbles until I no longer know what's in my reality and what's in another. The holiday postcard on the fridge flashes five different destinations. I clutch my ears and close my eyes.

They're just toy cars. They're just toy cars.

I pick up each death in my mind, look it over and consider a new thought. Despite experiencing them the way I do, I'm no expert in alternate realities. I'm not sure how they come about, how they split. Is it our decisions? Or probability? Or a mix of both? In this reality the coin comes down heads, you bring a gun to work; in another reality the coin comes down tails, you leave the gun at home. It's messier than that of course. If something happens in one reality, I don't know if it means it'll turn out exactly the same in this one. But what I do know is that in twelve other realities, I looked over the counter and copped it. And in this reality, I stayed hidden and got to live.

Another me gets a bullet through the counter. I dive round the fridge just as a bullet in this reality traces the same path.

Time to move.

The screaming subsides. Everyone's staying quiet – either hiding or dead. Footsteps are coming this way. Time to test my theory. I slip behind the next bank of desks just as another me, one who tarried, takes a shot in the leg then five in the chest. I rarely experience deaths outside of my personal space. It's always a near-miss – getting clipped by a train, hit by a falling brick, tripping on a loose paving stone – so I know that death was a close one. Sure, I have a front-row seat for 'what *not* to do' thanks to my less fortunate alternate selves, but how many near-misses can I afford?

The footsteps prowl closer. I hold my hand over my heart, as if I'm trying to keep it quiet and stop it bursting from my chest at the same time. I edge back and my ankle bumps into something wet and heavy. I make the mistake of looking. It's Caitlin, only there's deep red hole in the back of her head. I fall back and clap my hands over my mouth. Caitlin always makes the effort to talk to me at Friday night drinks. She breeds gerbils outside of work and listens to EDM while she codes. Who'll look after her gerbils now? The horror of her death is a black hole threatening to swallow me up. But I can't fall apart, not with the shooter so close.

It's just another death that doesn't belong to you.

I apologise to Caitlin and put her death into a toy car in my mind. I pick her up. Look at her. Then I put her back down and let her drive away.

The footsteps leave the room and I unclasp my hands from my mouth. I need a plan, a better one than waiting for my alternate selves to cop it like Schrödinger's canaries. Do I run? Do I hide? How long will it take for the police to get here? Five, ten minutes? Let's say it's going to take fifteen minutes before some sort of official task force arrives to deal with the situation. The gunman's skulking about, like he's looking for people. I picture him hunting for me among the desks. I wonder who it could be. Angus from Finance is always the brunt of jokes at staff parties. Or then there's Dafydd in Design with his hair-trigger temper. For some reason, I keep thinking of that guy from Support on the stairs this morning. What *is* his name? I briefly wonder if there's a reality where I remember his name and he doesn't shoot up our workplace. Probably not. Point is, it's only a matter of time until I'm found.

My best chance is to get out.

The next few minutes the office is a chess board with one terrifying queen and an infinite row of pawns that look just like me. The blockers have well and truly worn off and my senses are finely tuned. I've not felt this way in years. It's like I'm a military radar for my own demise and I'm picking up all of them in state-of-the-art HD. To keep my head straight I make a check list, as if I'm QA testing a website. Move too quickly. Bang. That's a bug. So, I take my time and think. Move too slowly. Bang. Another bug. So, I make sure I don't hesitate. Stop to help someone. They cry. Loudly. Bang. Bug again. I focus on saving myself. The self in this reality. All other deaths – both my alternate selves and the bodies on the floor – are just little toy cars whizzing through my head. I pick them up, then I put them down and let them run from me, until only I remain.

I die less. I get braver. That horrible staircase comes into view through the glass boardroom and I'm so close to this being over. After a shortcut through the cloakroom I scurry under the reception desk next to the large floor to ceiling windows emblazoned with our company logo. I can see the front door downstairs through the glass, but there are no blue lights out on the street. My heart sinks. The police should be here by now. It's been at least an hour, hasn't it? I check the clock opposite the desk. It's only been ten minutes. Ten minutes and I've died fifty times at least. That's a record I'm in no hurry to break.

I'm about to make my move, when footsteps round the corner. I duck down, hoping they don't see my reflection in the glass.

But it's not the gunman.

It's Fucking Linda.

Fucking Linda stands looking at the top of the stairs, a weird faraway look in her eyes. She doesn't look hurt, but she's standing out like a sore bloody thumb. Fucking Linda's going to get herself fucking killed. I think about this morning on the stairs, the kicked-dog look on her face, and guilt twists like a key in my gut. Maybe if I'm careful, we can both get out to safety. I quickly look about, then rise out of my hiding spot.

"Hey. Linds," I whisper as loud as I can.

She looks at me, surprised. God, she must be proper out of it.

"It's ok. I think he's still inside." I step toward her, offering my hand, "Let's get out of—"

Then I see the hunting rifle tucked under her arm.

Oh. Shit. *Fucking* Linda.

Three me's run. Bang. Two me's beg. Bang. Six me's throw something at her, a chair, a book, a bag. It doesn't matter. Bang. One me defiantly flips her the bird.

Bang bang bang.

Fucking Linda watches all of this flash across my face. She lowers her rifle. "Oh," she says, "Of course. You must be having a really bad day. How many times have you died so far?"

"Honestly, I lost count on the way to work," I say.

Fucking Linda fucking chuckles.

"I didn't really figure you into the plan." She braces the rifle back into her shoulder, "To be honest, I didn't know you had it so bad. You always seem so together."

I'm trying to come up with a game plan, but I've got nothing.

"I've got very good at pretending to be fine," I say.

Fucking Linda's face darkens. "I know what you mean."

I can see the clock on the wall above her head. Eleven minutes have passed. No other me's have died in a while. I just need to play for time.

"So, what's all this…" I gesture vaguely, "… about?"

The shooty end of the rifle is pointing straight at my gut.

"You know," she says, "Out of everyone here, I think you're the only one who truly understands what it's like."

She relaxes and the rifle's aim lowers to my thigh. If she misses the artery I could survive.

"What's what like, Linds?"

"Seeing the other you's." She leans forward, like we're just sharing office gossip. "Can yours see you back? I don't think mine can. I've only got the one, thank god. I tried talking to her when I was little, but she'd never say anything back. My parents thought I had an invisible friend."

Fucking Linda has the fucking Anxiety Gene.

"It was fine for a while. Just me and this other Linda living our lives in tandem. Brushing our teeth, playing with our toys. Then one day, we were studying for a test in school and I stopped and watched her. I think I just wanted to see what I looked like, so I watched while she studied. Of course, the next day I failed the test and she passed. That was the first time we'd ever differed."

I lean my head to one side like I'm listening and totally not counting down the seconds before the fuzz arrive.

"No need to panic, I thought. Just got to work a little harder and then I'll be right back on track. So, when the next test came I shut myself up in my room and studied all night long. And then I slept through the exam. I'd failed. Again. Meanwhile the other Linda, my potential, was racing away from me." For a moment her gaze traces some unseen horizon, before snapping back to me. "Can you follow yours? You know, if they go some place you're not. Can you see through their eyes?"

I shake my head. I'm too scared to speak.

14

"I can. It's a fucking curse. I'd watch her go on day trips with my parents and hang out with my friends, while I stayed in my bedroom struggling to catch up. But it was never enough. When I got an A on an essay, I could always see the A+ on hers."

Linda puts the rifle back under her arm.

"She's this celebrity thinker type person now. Married to a paediatrician. With a beautiful house and charming friends and her first child on the way. Do you know what torture that is? To have your perfect double showing you what your life could have been, while you're stuck living the consolation prize?"

Two minutes have passed. I nod sympathetically. Come on Linda, tell me more about your fucking awful life.

"She started maternity leave this week. She was lying in bed, looking through the cards from her colleagues, making plans for the future, and she was so..." Linda takes a big shuddering breath, "... happy. That's when I understood why there's only the two of us. I'm not supposed to compete with her." She pauses. "I'm supposed to balance her out. She's the charmed one and I'm-" she gestures at her rifle, "Well. I'm Fucking Linda. Aren't I?"

A cold feeling rises through my limbs. Fucking Linda is fucking insane.

"How does yours work again?" she asks, "Any time you die in an alternate reality you experience it here too? Is it like the uncertainty thing? Like, if I thought very seriously about shooting you in the stomach—"

Right on cue, an alternate me goes flying and I curl round my abdomen. Fucking Linda raises her eyebrows.

"Oh. Maybe you do have it worse."

I can't help myself. "You think?!"

Zero minutes. Fucking Linda's tired of fucking talking. She brings the gun back into her shoulder and aims straight at me. A shadow flits across the blinds behind her.

"On the stairs this morning, you looked so helpless. A little like you do now. Only I don't feel like helping this time." She shrugs. "Or maybe I do. Who knows? I'm feeling really indecisive lately."

The first wave of alternate bullets hit as Linda debates with herself whether or not she should shoot me. All the while, my alternate selves crumple to the floor over and over and over. I try to keep track of them all. I look them over and put them down, but they keep racing back to me, adding more each time until there are uncountable deaths around me, swirling like leaves in a hurricane. There are too many to pick up. Too many to feel separately. It's just a blur of pain and panic and terror.

So, I do the only thing I can think of.

I take all these deaths and I reduce them to one single idea. Death. My death, the one in my reality, the one that belongs to me, the one that *will* happen someday. I put death into a toy car and I look at it, without the comfort of a multiverse keeping it a whole other reality away. Then I set it down and I let it go.

And then, in that maelstrom of dying, like a word said over and over, death lost its meaning. And for the first time in years, I feel completely calm.

"Oh, so fucking what," I say. "You want to be remembered as this big scary monster? Fine. But did you have to be such a cliché? A shooting spree. Really? That's pretty basic, even for you."

Fucking Linda lets the barrel drop. She opens her mouth to say something, but I don't let her. It's my turn.

"Y'know, I've had nearly every flavour of death there is. Plane crash. Done it. Electrocution. Done it. Accidental beheading. Done it. Twice. This ride you've got me on, I've ridden it so many times I don't even bother picking up the souvenir photo anymore. I'm kind of a death connoisseur. And dying because my co-worker was too busy competing with her alternate self to succeed at her own goddamn life has got to be the dumbest one yet. Fine, shoot me. In a million other realities, a million other me's will have shaken it off by lunch time anyway."

Fucking Linda fucking falters. Not for long, but long enough.

"Oh fuck you—"

The sniper's bullet rips through her skull, spraying my face with her still-warm blood. Adrenaline courses through my veins as I watch Fucking Linda's headless corpse flop to the ground.

Black uniforms come piling into the building. I spread out my fingers. I can almost feel the pile of dead me's in a mound around my feet while I stand alone. The one who lives. I wipe the blood

16

off my face and step away from the carnage, forgetting the glass stairs behind me.

My foot slips. Fucking Linda's blood is all over the fucking floor and now it's slicked to the bottom of my boots. I try to find traction, but my foot slips again. Blue lights flash around me. My arms windmill.

No. Not the stairs, I think. *Not after all this.*

I teeter on the edge, a glass line between life and death, and a million other me's in a million other realities flinch.

Rhiannon A Grist is an award-winning Welsh writer of weird, dark and speculative fiction. Her Welsh folk horror, dark fantasy novella *The Queen of the High Fields* (Luna press, 2022) won Best Novella at the 2023 British Fantasy Awards. She lives in Edinburgh with her partner and far too many plants. Her debut horror novel Home Sick will be published by Solaris in 2026.
Anxiety Dream was first published in Shoreline of Infinity 14, 2019

THE
DREAM REPORTERS
Chris Kelso

It's always fascinating to see dream and memory mating in the primal waters of imagination. It will be an honour to witness Dechaume's union.

At the summit we see a great waste of desert. I'm surprised because this seems like such an obvious dream-metaphor for writer's block. Almost *too* obvious a metaphor for such a visionary writer like Dechaume – after all, it's a privilege being granted access to his inner creative kingdom. And Dechaume's historic contempt for journalists has not gone undocumented. We're certainly grateful, we just expected something a bit more original.

Anyway, we can't complain. Even if we have no success in fixing his writer's block, well, the advance money we received from the New York Times in exchange for the exclusive rights to our footage should tide us over nicely, for a time at least. I mean, this really is a once in a lifetime job.

I take a moment to document my peripherals on the hand-held dictaphone. I'm compelled to note everything for posterity. I feel seas of shifting mineral brush over my ankles and there is a peace here the kind of which I am wholly unfamiliar – the kind of calm that only the great Dechaume could imagine in all his ethereal genius. The sun sits as a great ghost ship marooned in the sky. Even in artistic limbo he can be breath-taking.

Then the shifting minerals change into something else. Something obscure, alien, and suddenly moving en masse. Hordes of insects appear, distinguished from obscurity by the sky's burning vessel. I tell John, my cameraman, to train the lens on the thick column of code-covered insects. This is classic Dechaume. His subconscious is trying to tell us something by stimulating the perceptual content around him. I sense we are edging closer to an explanation for his writer's block. The little dream-algorithms scurry in a northerly direction. Leading us, perhaps, to vital pieces of code that might complete the puzzle.

"We must be near a hot zone, John. Quick, turn up the fMRI resolution. Let's see where these things came from and what they're made of."

John complies and the temporal-res of the environment throbs with new creative activity.

"Creative neurons all right," – John confirms.

As documenters of Dechaume's private dreamscape, we have been trained to spot the obvious signs of subconscious communication, and as an accomplished oneironaut, Dechaume is theoretically with us every step of the way as a sort of lucid dream guide. And, *of course*, he stressed the importance of being present, metacognitively if not physically. We are exploring one of the preeminent voices of our generation. You can understand his sense of caution given that his mind is such a sought-after intellectual commodity. Our apparatus can achieve astonishing feats of tacit knowledge but trust is something you have to earn over time through hard work and loyalty. But it's clear Dechaume trusts us to some extent, if not unsupervised.

The insects scurry along the infinite drift and the viewfinder of John's camera glows with alluvium dreamscape.

New York Times, here we come!

I document to the listening dictaphone that this silent mud-cracked vista is a mute testimony to an intelligence far greater than our own. These affirmations are about posterity, sure, but they're also about keeping the grandmaster confident in our motives. We respect him and have no intention of exploiting him – and in dreams we are at our most vulnerable. If Dechaume starts feeling uneasy, he will eject us from his mind in a heartbeat. This job is all about relationships.

The winds of change sweep in from the west. I look up from the travelling insects and see the skeleton of some fallen behemoth laid before us.

"Are you getting this?" – I nudge John who brings the camera to eye level.

"What is it?" – he asks. I survey the half-buried fossils.

"Some relic of imagination. It's had its bones picked clean by some-*thing*. By *someone*."

The words are barely out of my mouth when I see a large spider emerge from behind the fractured birdcage of bone. I jerk back in fright. My Freudian education comes to the forefront – cigars, insects, spiders, fear, guilt.

Danger.

The arachnid scuttles cautiously down the left beam, taking sudden strides towards the colony of insects at our feet. The insects panic and try to disperse, screaming into sentience as the spider wraps its silk around the mass and consumes them in one foul movement of predatory engagement. Jaws flapping, acid spewing.

The screams of lost sentience.

"You know what this means?" – I turn to John, astonished.

"Oh, Christ…dream thieves?"

"Relax, this is an even bigger scoop!"

The Spiders.

John and I have heard of them. This is their calling card – spiders appearing from all corners to purge the algorithms of poor unsuspecting personal landscapes. All in the name of intellectual property fraud. It's easy money if you can infiltrate the right brain and utilise the right covert distractions. I'm starting to doubt if this desert is authentic. It's looking more like this desert is actually a front, an elaborate deceit created by these criminals to distract us.

I curse myself for failing to see through such flimsy camouflage.

But the emptiness shocks me. It certainly makes sense that these factions would target the most fertile imaginations of our generation, but Dechaume's mind has almost been entirely emptied of its creative content. I mean, they cleared the place out! Suddenly it occurs to me that John and I might be part of a much bigger conspiracy. A wholesale mind theft! My excitement dissipates and my next urge is to get out of Dechaume's head and regroup. Collect our data. Get more help. I turn to John but he is nowhere to be seen. The barren landscape starts bleeding like a Salvador Dali depiction of Cadaqués and my own form is soon as afflicted; my colours in quick deluge, hands pixelating to nothingness before my very eyes.

Blackness rushes towards me.

I'm being ejected from the dreamscape by Dechaume. *What is he doing? Is he panicking?* I can't collect my thoughts and I'm powerless. My limbs are stalks of wet spaghetti. The void sucks me into it and my shrieking heart roasts to a pulp in the microwave of my chest.

I release a silent scream…

When I come to, I'm lying supine in the sensory isolation booth. Heart racing, but no longer a mangled pulp. I get up and go to the adjacent chambers where the resting, dreaming bodies of John and Dechaume should be.

Both are gone, scalp electrodes floating in 2-inches of water.

I call after John but I have a feeling in my gut that he is either being held captive by The Spiders or was accidentally subsumed by Dechaume in his state of self-conscious panic. I go to the printer and see my dictaphone monologues stacked in a neat pile in the tray. I re-read some of my notes but they're all indecipherable algorithms. They've been converted to some kind of abstract neuro-algebra. So, the Spiders have scrambled my notes. The bastards. The New York Times will never accept this, especially without any live footage. I notice a footnote that reads in plain text, like an editor's additional comment –

'Weak premise for science fiction story about dream journalists and dream usurpers. Farfetched and convoluted. Characters are two dimensional, especially 'John' who was actually a double agent corrupted by The Spiders and sent to surreptitiously appropriate my thoughts anyway. The main character was so simple-minded that he didn't notice this betrayal. Back to the drawing board. More care next time.'

I hear the ominous scuttling of spider legs on dream-laminate.

Chris Kelso is a multi-translated writer, illustrator, and editor from Scotland. His work has been nominated for a British Fantasy Award, a Brave New Weird Award, and a Pushcart Prize. His latest collection of essays, 'On Melting: essays against the body' is out now from Control.

The Dream Reporters was first published in Vistas, Chris Kelso, 2021

A Cure for Homesickness

Anne Charnock

"You look rough," says her supervisor.

"Sorry. Self-inflicted. I didn't take my probe tablet this morning."

"*Jeez*. Why not?"

"Got distracted."

"Why didn't you say something?"

"Thought I could handle it." Helena drags her palms down her face. "I'm wiped out. Headache coming on."

"I could report you... Go back now. Take an early break."

She retraces her walking commute through the platform's labyrinth. A dose of daylight might help, she thinks, but there's no chance of that. At the end of her fifteen-hour shift at 2700 hours she'll catch the last sunrays out on the viewing deck. Together with her co-workers she'll drain a couple of beers and watch the

25

scintillating green sunset as it slowly calms and fades. Then there's Ray's farewell dinner, off-platform. Could be a late night.

She didn't bother with probe-and-fix tablets back home. Waste of money. Her mother pestered and even offered to pay. But what was the point? Helena could tell by the colour of her urine if she was boozing too much. And her weight wasn't exactly a problem. "Look, Mother, I know what I ought to do – a bit more exercise, drink more water, cut down on dairy. Save your money. I feel perfectly all right." Helena relented when this new job came up because taking the variant probe-and-fix medication was a condition of employment. "A plain physiological necessity," said the recruiter. "It's the only way anyone copes with a thirty-eight-hour day."

I'm an idiot, forgetting to take it this morning. As she trudges deeper beyond the administration decks and towards the personnel quarters, she wonders what her mother might be doing at this very moment. *What time is it back home?* She can never work it out.

She'll message her mother, she decides, at the end of today's shift and bring her up to date: debts paid off, and the cost of the return transport almost covered. *She'll be relieved for me.*

Helena takes the stairs two at a time. Her headache is thickening.

Lately she's considered extending her contract to help rack up her savings. Most people stay longer than they intended. *I'll broach the idea with Mother. See how she reacts.*

Eight years ought to be enough – eight *home* years, that is. She's done the maths, but she knows if she can just stretch to ten her wage-monkey days will be over.

And *then* she can focus on her health.

For the first time since she arrived six years ago, she recalls her mother singing a sea shanty in the kitchen. It *had* to be a Tuesday; she always baked on a Tuesday, however tired she felt. *Always scones and... That's unbelievable! I'd forgotten about her bread and butter pudding; my favourite. Come to think of it, the food here is kind of... disappointing. No, it's way worse than that!*

Helena is tempted to send an apology and cry off Ray's dinner this evening. The meal will be barely mediocre.

When was the last time, she wonders, that she truly enjoyed her food? She recalls a lunch she once had, way back, on holiday with... that cool guy. *What was his...?* Though she can't remember his name, she sees a white-clothed table on a cramped narrow veranda, which overlooks a steep wooded valley. She mouths the words, "Per primo, una zuppa di verdure per favore, di secondo, insalata di Cesari con Pollo, e da bere, vino bianco di Orvietto e una bottiglia di acqua mineral frizzante. Grazie." And, to herself, *I love Italy! Long lunches... under the shade of vines.*

Each footstep creates a shock wave that passes through her body and reverberates inside her skull. But she still manages to smile. *Those fields of sleepy sunflowers. And those crazy frescoes in...?* A green-faced devil eating a naked man, whole, head first. She places one hand on her head to dampen the pain.

Why these memories? God! I hope I'm not homesick.

On the final stretch towards her living quarters she detects a metallic smell with hints of synthetic freshener disguising staleness. An industrial smell, a hermetically-sealed-environment-type smell. She hasn't noticed it before. She lifts her right hand, pushes errant strands from her face and, fleetingly, she imagines a fresh salty breeze blowing along the corridor. She licks her lips.

As she opens the door to her windowless quarters she stalls and appraises the narrow steel-framed bed with its off-white bedding, the narrow desk – little more than a shelf – and the bare steel floor. *This isn't fucking minimal. It's dire.* She kicks a shoe across the room.

The probe-and-fix tablet lies by the sink. *So I did take one out of the bottle – no prize for that.* The tablet looks like a piece of hard shiny toffee but it tastes more like fudge. She swallows it without water and reaches for her toothbrush. A hesitation. She doesn't have time.

Out into the corridor, deserted at mid-shift, she takes long strides towards the first of many flights of stairs. As she takes her first step up, she halts. *William. He was called William.* And three steps higher she stops again. *It wasn't bread and butter pudding. My favourite was rice pudding with a burnt skin. Is she making rice pudding today? Is it Tuesday at home?*

Back at her workstation, Helena pulls up her day's assignment, deletes her earlier substandard work and starts from scratch. She feels no trace of a headache. *I feel better already. I'll not make that mistake again.* She kicks the table leg to check there's no knock-on pain inside her head. No. All clear.

In truth, she now admits to herself, she grew to like burnt skin on rice pudding only because Mother served it so often; an acquired taste born of repeated kitchen oversights. *Why didn't she ever set a timer?* She shifts in her chair so that her back is straight, her feet flat on the floor. *And William...nothing came of that little fling. Though Italy was lovely, except for the insect bites and those bloody noisy neighbours.*

Helena flicks her assignment aside and brings up her contract of employment. She finds the paragraph header: *Contract duration.* A few paces away, her supervisor looks up from a conversation and raises her eyebrows at Helena. She replies with a thumbs up.

Anne Charnock's writing career began in journalism and her articles appeared in New Scientist and The Guardian.

Her novel *Dreams Before the Start of Time* won the Arthur C. Clarke Award (2018). Her debut, *A Calculated Life*, was shortlisted for the Philip K. Dick Award and The Kitschies (2014), and The Enclave won the BSFA Short Fiction Award (2017). Anne's short stories and non-fiction have been published in anthologies including 2084 (2017), Best of British Science Fiction 2017 and 2020, and Writing the Future (2023).

Anne lives on the Isle of Bute, Scotland.

A Cure for Homesickness was first published in Shoreline of Infinity 11½, the Edinburgh Science Festival Special, 2018

Courie-in tae th Dark

Jeda Pearl

Wrap yersel in midnicht
Fauld-in moon-lickit whisker clouds
Crease Winter's solstice tae Beltane's dew
and kiss Midsummer's bountiful last licht

Drape Samhuinn's lively dusk ower heid and shoulder
Daunder on th slopes o heaven
Glide unner th glut o noctilucent nimbus

Courie-in tae th nae-knawin
Swing and dive intae undulatin mysteries
Sky, alive and divine, reflects yer dark matter back
It's okay you dinnae ken whit's gwan

Slip intae th eastern sunset
Swaddle yer mortality in nocturnal sustenance
Drink in th milk o dyin starlight
Th harmonies o th spheres are waitin

Wash yer face in cosmic gloam
Reminisce tae th throbbin dawin
Knit spindrifts o departin dark
and sleep, sated and cleansed, until morn

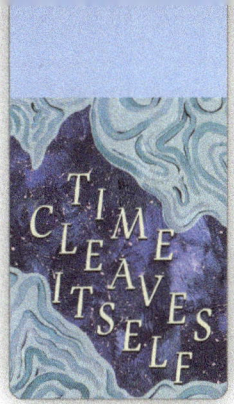

Jeda Pearl is a Scottish Jamaican writer.

In 2022, she was shortlisted for the Sky Arts RSL Award in poetry and longlisted for the Women Poets' Prize.

Her poems appear in art installations and several anthologies. Her debut poetry collection, *Time Cleaves Itself*, from which this poem is taken, is published by Peepal Tree Press

Time Cleaves Itself is available from www.shorelineofinfinity.com/shop/

The Worshipful Company of Milliners

T L Huchu

For as long as she could remember – one hour +/- – Kitsi had been in the factory. Before that, everything was bleak, blank, the foreboding ultra-darkness of non-existence. Like a baby gazelle, she had come to and wandered through the workshop floor aimlessly, skirting past milliners cutting felt, sewing and gluing. An arm reached out from behind her and touched her shoulder.

'New girl, you wanna come work with me?' said a smooth voice behind her. 'My name's Peshi.'

'Kitsi,' Kitsi replied, taking the four fingered hand offered, into her own.

'Always confusing for a first timer but don't worry, the fog will wear off in a bit.'

'Where are we?'

'Work, home, you choose what it is to you. Look around; these are all your sisters.' Peshi swept her arm in a grand arc.

All around were thin figures in uniform black dresses, much like French maids. Their faces resembled cat-human hybrids, feline eyes and round faces. Arms moved about furiously working, and watching them for a moment as they sewed and hewed, Kitsi felt an itch in her palm. She scratched and the itch grew worse until it became an unbearable burning engulfing her whole hand, spreading its necrotic pain upwards. She rubbed her palms together. Peshi handed her a pair of scissors and the itching stopped. It became a lukewarm glow in her fingers.

'Idle hands are the devil's workshop... you'll get used to the itch.' Peshi's tail came up over her shoulder and scratched her nose. She smiled, her mouth revealing sharp white teeth.

'Where am I?' Kitsi asked, taking a deep breath, confused by it all.

'Come, let's see what Boss Lady has in store for you,' she replied with a wink.

12 September 2008

I went to hunt the great white whale, and the Leviathan dragged me into the dark abyss. This is how it happens. You plunge the quill deep into your own heart. Query keyboard? Doesn't have the same stylistic flourish.

The thrill of defeat. Tried to capture that lightning in a bottle one more time. And time is an unkind mistress. Unknowable. Made up of the universe's flotsam, the great unwashed ocean full of plastic and elastic, bending, never breaking. But the Monster is torn out of my breast. Made out of my own rib. Grown and reared by my own hand. The same hand it bites: the same chest it pierces. From inside or out – the alien or the centurion?

A list of items left behind:

Carbon and other elements (see periodic table)

Debt and overdue mortgage

Manuscript of sorts

All my problems

Et cetera

It will happen like this, as in a story. I will go into my garage. Arrange my papers where you (the reader of this diary) will find them. But before you find them, you'll see me, a pendulum that has stopped swinging, hanging off the beam. For God's sake, DNR!

Then again...

Real life never pans out as the intricate clockwork of stories. Beginning. Middle. End. I've made my bed. Now lie.

The factory on Lobengula Road was cold in the winter and hot in summer. Its zinc metal roof was buckled and creaked with the slightest wind. What windows remained unbroken were caked in grime many decades old, like frosted glass, and the sunshine came in a yellowy brown texture full of dots and dark spots.

Kitsi stood on the dusty floor, her black boots surrounded by the debris and off-cuts strewn by the milliners. A languid fellow in overalls with dreadlocks and a cigarette dangling from the corner of his mouth walked around in a dream state with a large broom, sweeping through the rubbish, piling it at people's feet and in the corners of the room, creating small paths and never picking up after himself.

'We'll share this workstation,' said Peshi, drawing Kitsi out of her reverie. 'Keep it neat, keep it tidy. Do not lend our stuff to anyone. Never ever, ever. No one returns things around here.'

Someone from the next table tutted.

'Tools – scissors, needle, brush, pliers, pin pusher, spinner, corset stay, egg iron...'

'This is all too much to take in,' said Kitsi.

'Consider this your crash course.' Peshi kept on, pointing from one object to the next on their wooden worktop, gnarled and scarred from years of use.

Kitsi saw names etched out on the surface in desperate script, as though their owners didn't want to be forgotten. She ran her hand over a T, her slender finger falling into the groove. All around came the loud noise of snipping, hammering, voices humming or singing in the far corners of the factory floor. A large round clock near the main doors chimed with every hour and a cuckoo came out, jerky in motion as though the springs were broken.

'What if I can't do this,' Kitsi said.

'Easiest job in the world, you'll get the hang of it,' Peshi replied, her voice carefree and full of gusto. 'Cheer up. You're not the first to join the Sisterhood. Only we're not in London so…'

'But what if I really can't?'

'Oh dear.' Peshi stopped. Her fingers gripping a thimble like a croupier holding chips. 'This is what you were born to do. Boss Lady runs a tight ship around here. No hangers-on allowed. It's either in, or back to the void for you, and I certainly know which one I prefer.'

At the far corner of the table was a small forage cap in navy blue which Peshi was making. It was of the colonial style, soft sides with a firm round crown. The peak was made of black leather and bits of thread from the stitching jutted out. Peshi took it in hand and held it up.

'You have to be careful around here.' She leaned in closer and whispered, 'The sisters are not averse to borrowing now and again in order to keep their quota up.'

Kitsi learned the trade with the ease of a nestling learning to fly. Imitation, desperate flaps in thin air, a view of the dense undergrowth in which lurks all manner of predators, for with the fear of oblivion behind her, she had no choice in the matter. Her fingers, she found, were thin and nimble. She could thread a needle with ease and stitched up Peshi's work. A few times she pricked herself and drew warm red blood. She sucked her finger and went straight back to work.

Late in the morning, Peshi took a flask from a shelf under the worktop and told Kitsi it was time for a break. They both walked with a shuffling gait, each step no more than a few inches apart. From the back, they had the clockwork motion of geishas with bound feet, their tails swishing behind. Peshi stopped to introduce Kitsi to Fifi. They chatted for a moment, giggled like schoolgirls and moved on, out the creaking doors into the fresh air.

Kitsi took in the concrete pavement, cracked, with tufts of grass jutting out and litter blowing around. The fence was brown with rust and had more holes than wire.

Lorries coughed up smoke and droned along the road. The other industrial units were as dilapidated, many were worse. Roofs caved in. Machinery stolen and looted for scrap.

Near the gate sat an old security guard reading the *Daily News*.

'Don't know why they have him,' said Peshi, lighting a cigarette. 'The humans can't see us anyway.'

'How long have you been doing this?' Kitsi asked.

'Long enough to know enough not to care. Fancy a cuppa?' Peshi poured a drink into the cap of her flask. 'It used to be teaming around here, back in the day. Queues of trucks brought in bales of cotton and left with reams of cloth. Logs from Manicaland were pulped and became paper and timber. You could smell new rubber in the air from the tires and tubes manufactured around the corner. Early in the morning you had the wind chime of bottles rattling on the backs of Coca-Cola trucks, behind which came Lobels' laden with bread. They did everything, cement, plastics, you name it. These streets were always packed with labourers going to and fro. It's another world all together now.'

A woman carrying a dish of *masawu* fruit on her head and a baby on her back walked past on the desolate road. Kitsi tried to imagine this place as it had been in the past but could not. Their factory cast a sad shadow on them. She turned to see its worn bricks, the broken sign that said *Mahendere Textiles* with a picture of a hand, thumbs up, next to it.

Peshi finished her cigarette and crushed it with the sole of her boot.

'Come on. Let's get back inside,' she said.

10 September 2001

Things will never be the same again. This thing, this Monster, this tyrant, has me by the throat and won't let go.

Imagine. A man pierced in his breast by a knife. It (the knife) causes him untold pain and misery. As he lies on the ground, his arms cradle the knife, almost lovingly, gently. He knows if he tries to remove it, he'll bleed out into the earth and surely die. In this moment, the knife is at once his tormentor and his saviour.

This sweet, beautiful idea. There can be no fault in this idea. If there is a fault, it is that it is perfect. In an imperfect universe, perfection is fault. But we are drawn to it, like mystics of old. Where there is darkness, let me be light. And light like a candle or stars consumes the object that creates the light. The giver of the gift is simultaneously destroyed by it. Does this make any sense?

Each new sentence I craft. Every time my finger presses on the keyboard, transmitting an electric signal towards the white page. I commit an atrocity. I move further and further away from that perfect idea. I am a builder with no cement or spirit level. Every new brick I lay drives me towards ruin. To counteract this, I redraft and rewrite, I lie to myself that each draft leads to more perfect sentences – as if there can ever be such a thing! But accept that premise. The question then becomes: is a book full of perfect sentences a perfect embodiment of the Idea, *or is it merely solipsistic self-aggrandisement?*

After a few weeks, Kitsi felt as though she was not actually learning from Peshi. The trade came to her like something remembered from a long time ago. It was in her blood. Peshi would show her a stitch or technique and within moments she had grasped it, her hands moving with the hesitant confidence of an old pro come out of retirement.

They had a box full of hats when one of the messenger-boys came to their table. He was short, less than three feet tall, and wore khaki shorts, a starched white shirt with brass buttons and a pith helmet that overwhelmed his head. He looked every bit the colonial servant, shiny brown shoes and a pristine moustache, and he even saluted the milliners, too.

'Tell us where to take 'em and we'll do it for you and do it right, sister,' he said.

'Not a chance,' Peshi replied with a laugh.

The messenger-boy stood on the balls of his feet and stretched up as high as he could, an extra inch or two.

'Come on, sister, that's not fair, is it?' he said in a gruff voice.

'Never trust them,' Peshi said to Kitsi. 'They mix the orders up, give hats to the wrong people and leave chaos in their wake.'

'Reorganised the order, we have! Reliable like DHL, now.' the messenger-boy replied.

'That's what you say every time and then you mess it up again. Come on, Kitsi, we'll deliver these ourselves.'

The messenger-boy snorted, clicked his heels together and gave a salute. He turned and went to the next station to solicit someone else.

'You've hurt his feelings,' Kitsi said.

'They have thick hides. And trust me, you don't wanna try them. Always make sure when you work, you're quick enough to leave a bit of time to deliver your own hats. The messengers are alright most of the time, but when they cock-up, they do it in grand fashion with fireworks, explosives and singed eyebrows.'

Kitsi carried the box of hats, while Peshi followed with an armful of brown files.

'Wait,' Peshi said. She reached down and picked up two runners, put one in her apron pocket and gave the other to Kitsi. 'Take this with you. You'll need it when the itch comes.'

They went past busy workstations, other milliners toiling at their craft. Peshi reached out with her tail to touch Kitsi's and they walked on the floor tail in tail. She had a smile on her face and a spring in her step.

They reached a door with a fire exit sign on the lintel and walked into a long wide white corridor, brightly lit by incandescent bulbs. There was a queue of messenger-boys in front of them as they patiently waited their turn. When they were near, Peshi turned to Kitsi:

'Make sure you're nice to the master of the gate, otherwise he'll send you around the planet a dozen times before you get back.'

The master of the gate was an older messenger-boy sat on a stool, with a full beard that reached past his knees and dangling feet to the floor. He wore a grand coat with epaulette on his shoulders and many medals on his chest. In his right hand he held a lever which he pulled from time to time.

'And where are you off to this time?' he said to Peshi.

'Just taking the new girl out for a spin.'

'Deliveries are best left to the professionals, you know.'

'But if I did that, how would I ever get to come here to see your handsome face?' Peshi replied. The master of the gate broke out into a toothless grin. She handed him a pouch of chewing tobacco.

'Well, tell me where you want to go,' he said, smiling still.

'Accra, Lubumbashi, Ankara, Ljubljana, Edinburgh, Salem, Xiamen and back home again.'

'You have to get the order right, that's the quickest way. Lubumbashi before Accra then out to Ankara.'

'That's why you're the best, but leave Edinburgh for last,' Peshi said walking into a room the size of a small closet.

'Demand, demand, that's all you lot do! Mess with my poor old head. So, it's Accra to Ljubljana and from there east until you get back.'

Kitsi took a deep breath and watched as the doors closed. It was dark inside. She held the box tight against her breast. 'Brace yourselves,' the master called from outside. She heard a cranking sound and then the floor below them seemed to buckle, then they were falling through a black hole, fast, faster and faster, the wind running through their hair. Kitsi closed her eyes and screamed and screamed; Peshi screamed with her, high pitched like a cat. Then they hit something hard and fell to the ground. She opened her eyes and she was on a pavement outside a grand building with Dutch style arches.

'Welcome to Lubumbashi,' Peshi said, getting up and dusting her dirty uniform.

The sky was bright blue and the sun above fierce. Cars drove bumper to bumper, and people walked past them without noticing. They walked into an office, up to the first floor, where they found a man at a desk, working on a spreadsheet on a computer. The fan above him spun lazily.

'This is Katumbe Kafue,' she said, leaning over his shoulder and peering at the figures he had on Excel. 'How boring; give me the yellow and red kippah in the box... That's the one.' Peshi held it up. 'I love your stitching by the way.'

'But he's not Jewish,' Kitsi said.

'Jewish smewish.' Peshi placed the hat on Katumbe's head. He paused and leaned back in his seat. He rapped his fingers on the desk. After a minute or two, he returned to his spreadsheet. Peshi smiled and said, 'His first manuscript was rejected everywhere. Soon, he'll make his second attempt.'

They found a cleaning closet in the building, full of smelly chemicals and stinky mops. Kitsi stomped the floor three times with her left foot and soon they were falling through space. They landed in Accra where they gave a student her first baseball cap. In Ljubljana they gave an old man a boater with bright green ribbons on it.

It was late at night when they landed in Salem. Here they found a woman, Maria Hernandez, sleeping in a single bed. Kitsi watched her curled up like a foetus, under a sheet, snoring lightly.

'I always come to her in her sleep,' Peshi said.

They gave Maria a multi-coloured beanie hat, and as soon as it touched her head, she sprung up, swung her feet onto the floor and marched to her desk. Maria lit her lamp, picked up a notebook and began to scribble in it. Peshi placed her hands on Maria's shoulders, stood for a moment to watch her write, and then kissed her on both cheeks.

'You can't help but fall in love with them,' Peshi said.

Soon they were travelling around the world again. It was drizzly when they wound up in Edinburgh at a small park in Stockbridge. Pine trees filled the air with their sweet scent and a man sat on a bench, staring at the falling raindrops. Kitsi felt her heart skip a beat.

He was ragged; stubble grew on his cheek a few days old. His hair needed cutting, the coat he wore was wet from the rain, but he sat with his brown eyes transfixed to a point far off in space.

'He's yours,' Peshi said. She took out a file and gave it to Kitsi. His name was Jonah Mangirazi.

Kitsi felt drawn to him with the longing of a long lost lover. She curled her hands tightly around the runner, for the itch had overcome her. The tool felt nice and cool in her palms.

'Come closer, he won't bite,' said Peshi, standing next to the man. 'Isn't he just so intense?'

Kitsi could not speak, there was a lump the size of an orange in her throat.

'This one is a *mambara*. He hasn't written a single word in four years. He's rejected everything that's come his way,' said Peshi.

'Why?' Kitsi asked feebly.

'Who knows? I want you to study his skull, how broad and fierce it is. Our craft is half phrenology. You must study the head to make the right hat.'

Kitsi took out a tape measure from her apron pocket. She approached Jonah and measured the size of his skull. She noted peculiarities, the prominent occiput, thinning hair, everything about him fascinated her.

'It's up to you to make him a hat that fits,' said Peshi.

There was nothing but utter joy and warmth in Kitsi's heart as she set out to make a hat for Jonah in the workshop. She chose the finest materials and worked day and night, every thought, her entire will, bent to making him the best hat she could. She put everything she knew into it and created a fine herringbone trilby, grey trimmings, with a black ribbon around the crown. Kitsi felt it had mystery and allure to it, something a hero in a noir movie would wear.

6 September 1998

I was walking along the river. Like an eclipse, it came to me. Covering everything. Eureka!

This is how it happened. I was walking, one foot after the other – like I always do and it came to me.

Like the annunciation. It felt divine. Dear Diary, I know I sound crazy. But that's how it happened.

I was walking along the river. Boom. A flash of white light. Maybe a soft whisper from over my shoulder.

The truth is. If I am to tell it straight. It doesn't feel like it came from me at all.

In the corner of my eye. It was there all along, like that itch that comes just before you sneeze.

I was walking along the river. In that moment, all I wanted was to get back to my office in my little garage.

The entire factory floor, except for the loom in the middle, went quiet when the Boss Lady's door swung open, banging against the wall. Her office was up on the first floor. It had large windows looking down on the floor; a series of metal steps led to up it. Boss Lady's shoes clanked as she descended the stairs to the bottom, where a messenger with a large laundry bag was stood at attention, waiting for her.

Like the milliners, she was feline, but bigger, curvier, more buxom like a bobtail. Her tail swished this way and that as she walked, as if to purposefully take up more space. She wore an elegant green *kaba* of handmade *aso-oke* fabric, interlaced with fake emeralds that reflected light against the swirling patterns. It had puffy sleeves which made her look grand, and on her head she wore a stylish *gele*, of similarly exuberant green, looking like a ring of concentric halos flowing outwards. Though she'd tied it herself, it had the gravity defying wizardry of a Segun Gele original.

'Many more returns this month compared to last month,' Boss Lady shouted in a shrill voice. 'Production is down 0.5%.'

A collective groan went out across the factory floor.

'At this rate, we'll have to lay off a few souls. Why can't we be more daring, like computer games?' she said.

There were many anxious faces around the workstations as she weaved round them, stopping here to give a return, and there to issue stern admonishment. She was firm and business-like in every movement, not a gesture was wasted. She complained about the cost of materials, untidy stations, the state of the floor, missing equipment, nothing escaped her keen eye.

Kitsi and Peshi tensed up as she reached their station.

'And this one is yours?' Boss Lady said to Kitsi, fishing the trilby out of the laundry bag. Kitsi nodded.

'She's new,' said Peshi.

'No one is talking to you, little Miss Bigmouth,' Boss Lady replied. From this close, Kitsi saw the freckles on her cheeks and across the bridge of her nose. 'Kitsi, I want you to look at the wrinkles in this felt. You didn't stretch it enough over the hat block. Make sure you steam it well. Look at this brim, ghastly. Does that look even to you? Learn to eyeball when you cut, if you can't then measure and mark.'

Tears welled up in Kitsi's eyes. She shook with emotion. To see her work returned like this caused her so much pain.

Boss Lady lowered her voice. It became gentle, maternal even: 'You do know you only have two chances left. We'd hate to lose you.'

Boss Lady passed by, the messenger-boy in tow.

Kitsi felt Peshi's tail on her shoulder. She brushed it off and buried her face in her hands.

'It's going to be okay. No one ever gets it right the first time,' Peshi said.

'I did,' a voice said from behind them. It was Fafi, Peshi's arch-rival. She walked tall and confident. 'Look newbie, maybe you ought to think about finding a new master.'

'Be careful,' Peshi said, almost a growl.

'She hasn't told you, has she?' Fafi ignored her. 'All her little apprentices this year have failed and gone back to the void. That never happens at my table. Think about that and come join me if you want. I'm right in the corner, table number 23.'

Fafi turned and left, her tail erect, high up above her head.

'Poacher,' Peshi said.

In the middle of the factory floor stood an old loom. Beside it sat the most beautiful woman in the room, fully human in her form. She had smooth black skin, dark as polished gabbro. Sweat glistened on her face like diamonds caught in sunlight. She wore a loose silk dress and jewelled choker around her neck and sat with her back straight. A basket of Panama straw lay at her feet, waiting to be woven.

She was the last remaining muse in the factory. No one knew her name. Once she worked here with her sisters, but they had all gone away, moved into television or video games. Alone, she

42

seldom paid attention to the milliners, but now she looked up from her work, saw Kitsi crying and frowned.

Kitsi ran away to the off-cuts room. She locked herself inside and ignored Peshi pounding on the door. There were three sets of doors at the front wall of the factory, near the foot of Boss Lady's stairs. The other two led to the materials room and the canteen.

The power went off as Kitsi sat on the cold floor of the room, surrounded by scraps of fabric whose glorious colours she'd seen in the blur of her tears. She felt the unbearable shame of failure loping through her stomach like a swarm of cockroaches. Boss Lady's voice was in her head, prodding every tiny error in her work.

She lay down on the floor and her head touched something hard. She picked it up, her hands tracing it, and its dimensions felt like those of an old book. Clutching it to her chest, she closed her eyes and dreamt of a new hat.

When Kitsi finally woke up, she was ready to create something new, something really special this time. She had to if she wanted to survive.

3 August 1998

As you brush against bodies your left hand weighed down by Gap shopping bags full of useless things you feel nothing in your right pause and in that instant you turn behind you and ask where is he where is he he was here just a moment ago and now there's nothing just heads and bodies in designer clothing going into and out of designer shops not noticing the hen franticly searching in the undergrowth for her chick where moments ago she saw the shadow of an eagle flying high above and cried out which is you in that mall where is he where is he he was here just a moment ago in and out of shops you go searching for him in changing rooms under shelves calling out his name again and again not caring that you look mad up the escalators and down again into Next Debenhams Hollister Waterstones running your high heels cluttering on the hard granite floor lit up by florescent lights it all seems so large and big and insane a labyrinth you should never have come here never have let go of a security guard stops to ask if he can help where is he where is he

The second failure made Kitsi feel like she was drowning in a vat of sticky molasses, every pore glued shut, unable to breathe and to move. Fafi took to passing by her workstation and winking at her two, sometimes three, times a day. The urge to defect to save herself was there, but Kitsi chose to be loyal even if it meant her own life. When she walked, the sisters averted their gaze, as though she was the host of an incurable ailment.

Peshi decided to take Kitsi away from the factory to clear her head. The place ran 24/7 and the milliners never had time off – at least not officially. They walked tail in tail and entered the master's porthole and wound up on George Street in Edinburgh.

They bought cups of coffee from a café on the street. Well, they didn't exactly buy them – when you're invisible, you can just take stuff. All they had to do was wait for the barista to make the right order, turn his back for a moment and one touch, it vanished; then when it left their hands, it reappeared as trash in exactly the same spot it was 'borrowed' from.

They walked west to Charlotte Square where white tents were erected for the Festival.

Kitsi noticed a lot of people milling about in fine hats, some of which she immediately realised had been made by the Worshipful Company of Milliners in their little factory in Harare. It was easy to differentiate their hats from the normal human hats. For a start, their clients seldom wore clothes to match the hat for they were unaware they had it in the first place, and there was a certain aura which marked their handiwork.

'If only you'd been here last year. I would have taken you to Abekouta in Nigeria for the Ake Festival. My, you should have seen what hats they wore!' said Peshi excited in the warm summer air. 'Their *geles* put Boss Lady to shame.'

'How long have you been doing this?' Kitsi asked. She was melancholic.

'Since 1969. My first writer was David Maillu from Kenya. I still make his hats,' Peshi replied wistfully.

The iron railings outside the square were papered with posters advertising shows. Crowds went through the gates, past the reception with shelves of free guides and rows of ticket stalls to the left. They walked into the gardens, on an open grassy square where many chairs had been placed. People sat in the sun, drank alcohol and read books. Kitsi and Peshi ensconced themselves on some deck chairs.

'If anyone tries to sit on you, poke them up the arse with your finger,' Peshi said. She reached into her apron pocket and took out her runner, for the itch had come upon her.

'Do you ever wish you were free like them?' Kitsi asked, watching at the humans wandering around.

'What makes you think they *are* free?'

'Their lives are not tied to some grimy factory like ours.'

'You have much to learn. They have their own petty issues and struggles, just like we do. Every day is a battle for them, as it is for us. The writers especially are slaves to their craft. No one is absolutely free. We all are what we are and how we make the best of it is what defines who we are.'

They were close to the bookstore but couldn't see within because there was a long queue of people, winding round, waiting to see the author of an extremely popular fantasy series. Peshi pointed out a writer wearing Somi's wide brimmed cavalier hat, which had a red ribbon and blue ostrich plume tucked in.

More writers walked in and out of the green room. Kitsi liked a purple stovepipe hat worn by an austere-looking woman, which Peshi said was made by Anami. Behind her was a tall man in a sombre black suit who wore a frivolous yellow cocktail hat on the right side of his head, complete with a veil. Peshi sniggered.

'That's why I told you not to trust the messenger-boys,' she said. 'He's Neville Sutton, a writer of very *serious* literary fiction. Now, someone gave him a romance hat, his new novel is, I swear, Mills and Boon to the core, yet critics fall over themselves, raving about how profound it is. "An acute expression of the human condition".'

'I think he looks lovely in that hat.'

'Oh, look, here's one of mine,' Peshi pointed at a woman in jeans and a t-shirt who wore a leopard skin headband with many feathers. 'She writes gritty feminist novels and I gave her a Zulu *impi's* headgear. You gauge your writer – are they a peacock or a mole or something in between? – and then you make the hat to fit. It doesn't matter what sex they are, so long as it's the right one for them.'

That afternoon they lounged and drank pot loads of coffee, watching their sisters' creations: cloches, kufi caps, ten-gallon hats, garbos, hennin, Pende beaded crowns, shakos, turbans, Himba ekoris, all manner of creations in wild colours and styles, some of which they couldn't even name. It was one thing for Kitsi to see them in the factory, but out here in the real world, it was dizzying and dazzling. For the milliners, writers at a festival were models on a catwalk. And every now and again, she saw a writer whose head was far too large for their hat.

Kitsi shut herself in the off-cuts room. There were tall shelves full of little bits of material of different forms and sizes in transparent tubs. Under a pile of cloth, she retrieved the album and began to look at the pictures within. The dust from the book clung to her hands. In it she saw hats of such exuberance and dare, she could not believe they could have been made here, or anywhere for that matter.

She was so engrossed that she didn't notice the door open and a tall figure loom, watching her. A voice startled her:

'I was wondering where that went.'

Kitsi was startled and dropped the album. It was the muse, leaning against the doorframe, her arms folded. Her long afro brushed against the top of the frame. She hid one hand behind her back and smiled at Kitsi.

'You should have seen this place when my sisters worked here. In those days we made such marvels as you cannot imagine, child. We hatted poets in the Arab lands, Russian novelists whose work is without equal, French satirists, started Anglo Sci-Fi, whispered to West African myth makers, gave dreams to Shona storytellers, we did them all.'

'Why did you stop?' Kitsi asked, closing the album.

'My kind is fickle. Film came in, then television, then video games; my sisters all moved to America or Japan. Why else do you think those forms exploded while your art withers?' the muse sighed. 'I stayed on but couldn't do it myself. Luckily, or not, the universe abhors a vacuum. I was alone in this place when the first of your kind popped up and took her place at a station. Soon you'd infested the place like rats and we had post-modern grotesques all over the place. The beginning of the end if you ask me. Thank God my sisters left material and some basic designs, otherwise who knows what other travesties you lot would have wrought upon the world.'

Kitsi stood up, walked over to the muse, and offered the book back. Unable to meet her eye to eye, she looked down at the muse's feet which were in simple rubber soled sandals with *rekeni* straps.

'You keep it, child. The milliner's existence is fragile, she pops into being as she is needed, and out of it when she's no longer useful.' the muse said and not without some sadness. 'Yet from the moment you arrive you are fully formed with speech and knowledge, almost as though you're recycled, no reincarnated. I pity your lot. Take this.' From behind her back, she brought out the most elegant woven Panama straw, painted with varying shades of yellow and orange.

'It's beautiful,' Kitsi said, afraid to touch it.

'Take it. It's yours, child, and good luck to you.'

The muse left her in the room and within a minute Peshi rushed in, begging to be told what had happened. This was the first time any of them had seen the muse get up to walk, let alone speak with one of them. Kitsi went back to work and made the best hat she could.

22 June 1998

I knock my head against the wall. I take drugs. I take long meandering walks. Imagine the plumber who can't come into work on Monday because he has plumber's block!

Where do our ideas come from? No, that makes it sound too hocus-pocussy. As if they're drawn from the ether. It's not that I don't have ideas, it's just everything I think of is too pedestrian. Not daring enough. Been done before, by someone else, better.

What if I lack the genius required? Nonsense. Writing is carpentry, there's no magic in that. Instead of wood we use words. Allusion to St. Joseph. Father. Protector. Cuckold. Loose connections.

I try to think, to conjure it up, but nothing comes to me. Maybe I try too hard. Hit the library. Hit the gym. Hit myself. Give it time, it will come. And if I'm just not good enough? Shame! Fuck it.

When power went off during the day, the factory was dim, but the sisters went on with their work regardless. Pigeons fluttered their wings and cooed as they roosted on the metallic roof struts above. Kitsi no longer had to work now, though she helped Peshi from time to time. All she could do was wait for the verdict on her last hat. Her neck was stretched out on the guillotine, waiting for the blade to swing down. She stood near the left wall and read the names inscribed, one to a brick, in crayon. These were the novices that didn't make it, some of their names too faded to be legible, then as she got further up the wall, no more names, just Xs. They'd done that because space was running out. Kitsi realised that if she returned to the void, all that would be left would be an X and nothing more. The other sisters averted their eyes as she wandered between the worktops, checking out new designs. Nanomi was creating her trademark seed hats, each the size of an acorn, which sprouted and grew into awesome creations once they touched the writer's scalp. But none of these wonders did anything for Kitsi's humour. She decided to go out and take a walk, hand in hand with her fear, along the Mukuvisi River, for her fate was now irredeemably out of her hands.

7 April 1998

Every Tuesday and Thursday, without respite, I commit an act of fraud. Let's define some terms via the Oxford Dictionary:

Fiction: (late middle English (in the sense 'invented statement'): via Old French from Latin fictio(n-), from fingere 'form, contrive'. Compare with feign and figment.) **Something that is invented or untrue.**

Fraud: (middle English: from Old French fraude, from Latin fraus, fraud- 'deceit, injury'.)

A person or thing intended to deceive others, typically by unjustifiably claiming or being credited with accomplishments or qualities.

Notice how the two words are near synonymous. And that's what I do standing in front of my students every Tuesday and Thursday, without respite. I peddle empty words and they lap them up like sponges. When I was a child I liked stories – every child likes stories. I'd sit on my grandma's lap and order her to tell me ngano. *As soon as she was finished, I would order her to tell it again. I could listen to the same story a thousand and one times and, each time, enjoy it just as much as I did during the first telling.*

Kitsi decided if she was going down, she'd do it style. From the muses' album she'd seen the hats of the masters; Dostoevsky's grey and black cloches with small intricate labyrinths, like brain gyri and sulci, and Tolstoy's large multi-coloured sombreros, packed with figurines of people, animals, machines of war, grand in scope and ambition.

She had the muse's elegant straw and set about doing her work. Peshi was not allowed to help her, she was on her own, those were the rules. Each breath Kitsi took smelt of the glue used by the pot load in the factory.

She wet the straw thoroughly and was glad to see the paintwork didn't run or ruin. The straw was light and soft to the touch and bendy. She placed it on a hat block and gently stretched it out. Nothing she'd used before felt so malleable; as though her thoughts transmitted themselves perfectly into the shallow crown she created to fit off-centre, on the left side of the head.

The brim Kitsi made was a large disk, exuberant like the rings of Saturn. She could feel the sisters' eyes watching her work with this beautiful material as she trimmed the border and sewed black ribbon there.

She made a red rose, stuck it on the side of the crown, and, within, inserted embracing figurines, male and female. Then she glued tiny straw poles with stars on either end. Inside the hat she inserted soft white cotton lining, marked out with the graffiti from the Roman alphabet.

The muse passed by her table and gave her a little wink.

Kitsi found Jonah pensively walking along the Water of Leith with his two dogs. As she placed the hat on him, it blocked the sun over his head, leaving him in the grip of its shadow. He froze: a sybaritic look of horror stencilled on his face.

3 March 1998

Subjective assertion: I am a sick man.

Everything's fucked! End of the world type calamity – mass extinction event, cancel Christmas, hope you bought insurance. On mornings like this I fear I'll be revealed as the fraud that I am. Fantastic new review from Michelle Kodaof the Times. *The book is two years old and they're reviewing it again! What the fuck?*

Sold 15000 copies – 14446 to be exact.

Hardly going to shake the world is it? It's cold and bleak in adulthood and no one gives a crawling fuck. The signs are there in the stars; you just need a kaleidoscope. Last week I did a festival in Glasgow and was shocked people even bothered to turn up to my event. The fucking moderator hadn't even read my work. Regurgitated the same list of clichés.

The novel is dead/dying. So it goes.

The messenger-boy came with news of the manuscript, a full decade after Kitsi had made her hat. No milliner had ever had to wait that long for ascension.

Kitsi gave a tired smile, but it turned into a grimace when the messenger-boy told her of Jonah's end.

'It's my fault,' she said to Peshi.

'Don't blame yourself, they do that sometimes,' Peshi replied. 'All that matters is that you made it.'

'An evil trade, my life for his.'

'The universe is built on trade-offs.'

The sisters gathered around Kitsi, even Fafi gave a half-hearted word of congratulations. Boss Lady descended from her office. She made a speech about the labour of creation, the part the milliners played in preserving a dying art, and she inducted the newest milliner into the Worshipful Company.

Like all before her, Kitsi received a pair of white gloves and copper scissors to the applause of the Sisterhood.

She curtsied and turned to her workstation. The factory was filled with ululation and song, the noise echoed off the zinc metal roofing. Kitsi didn't feel joy; instead she had the full awareness of the terrors that lay ahead, the hats to be made.

T.L. Huchu's work has appeared in Lightspeed, Interzone, Analog Science Fiction & Fact, The Year's Best Science Fiction and Fantasy 2021, Ellery Queen Mystery Magazine, Mystery Weekly, The Year's Best Crime and Mystery Stories 2016, and elsewhere.

He is the winner of a Hurston/Wright Legacy Award (2023), Alex Award (2022), the Children's Africana Book Award (2021), a Nommo Award for African SFF (2022, 2017), and has been shortlisted for the Caine Prize (2014) and the Grand prix de l'Imaginaire (2019).

Tendai also guest edited Shoreline of Infinity 18, the BAME special issue.

The Edinburgh Nights series is now on its third instalment.

Find him @TendaiHuchu

The Worshipful Company of Milliners was first published in Interzone 257, 2015

Armata: A Fragment, by Thomas Erskine

Noel Chidwick

Thomas Erskine is likely to be the first Scot to have written a science fiction novel. It's called *Armata: a Fragment* and was published in 1817.

Thomas Erskine, 1st Baron Erskine, (10 January 1750 – 17 November 1823) was a British lawyer and politician who served as Lord Chancellor of the United Kingdom between 1806 and 1807 in the Ministry of All the Talents.

In his retirement, as well as fighting for animal rights, Greek independence, and the defence of Queen Caroline, he wrote Armata, a strange tale of a man sailing to the moon upon a highway of ocean.

Armata was published a year before Mary Shelley's Frankenstein...

Erskine was born in a tenement at the head of South Grays Close on the High Street in Edinburgh – near the Museum of Childhood, if you're looking for the site.

He has a full Wikipedia entry: he seems to have been a busy chap, in the same mould as John Buchan. If you want to read Armata, you can do so at the Public Domain Review, where they have a full scan of the original book. I haven't found an edition yet of a typeset version – work is beginning on an edition to be published by Shoreline of Infinity/ SF Caledonia

A R M A T A:

FRAGMENT.

Erskine, Thomas Erskine, Baron

SECOND EDITION.

LONDON:

JOHN MURRAY, ALBEMARLE STREET.

1817.

INTRODUCTION.

WHEN Galileo discovered the phases of Venus through his telescope, he was cast into prison by the tribunal of the Inquisition.—He was cast into prison, as Milton, in his Areopagitica has well described it, only for differing in astronomy from the Franciscan and Dominican monks.— Imperfect as the state of science was in the age of that great philosopher, it was nevertheless believed to be at its fullest maturity, and it has always been so considered, from Noah's flood to the present hour: the pride of man will scarcely enable him to accept the most manifest evidence of his senses, when brought into collision with the most manifest errors which time has sanctioned; and until ignorance shall be fairly pushed from her stool by the main force of truth, she will continue to sit staring like an

B

still not subtending any angle to the naked sight, while others of our hemisphere appeared more distant, and some I missed altogether; but the moon, full orbed, was by far the most striking object, appearing much larger than with us, and her light, though borrowed, proportionally resplendent.

I shall not attempt to describe my astonishment at this sublime and hitherto super-human spectacle, because having been in all latitudes, and being, as I have already said, familiar with astronomy in its abstrusest branches, I was now fully convinced, not only that I was in no part of the world ever visited before, but that there was something else belonging to the world itself never even known or imagined. I am well aware that the figure and extent of our planet can neither be denied nor doubted; the moon, whilst I am writing, is just touching the sun's vertical disk within a second of calculated time, and moving onward to predicted eclipse; and in my voyage homewards, I saw her at the

the foretold moment wading into the earth's shadow, and at last totally obscured.—The revolutions round our axis and in our orbit mock in their precision the most celebrated inventions by which the astonishing art of man has contrived to measure even their shortest periods; and as the fixed stars, from wherever seen upon our earth, must be uniformly visible in the same positions and magnitudes, I could account, *at the moment*, in no other way for the position of the ocean in which I now found myself, than by supposing we had a ring like Saturn, which, by reason of our atmosphere, could not be seen at such an immense distance, and which was accessible only by a channel so narrow and so guarded by surrounding rocks and whirlpools, that even the vagrancy of modern navigators had never before fallen in with it; they having always hitherto been sent back, like other vagrants, to their original settlements. An unsurmountable objection; however, after a little attention, soon opposed itself to the theory of this sea being on such a ring; because, though from an idiot, worshipping the shapeless phantoms of her own blind creation. This is so universally true, that even in this æra of comparative light, I expect, *for a season at least*, to find but little credit for my discovery of a New Land, because I cannot lay down its position on any accredited map; geographers having decided and certainly *almost* supported by the fact, that we know as perfectly every spot of *considerable magnitude* upon the earth, as I can now see the dots over the i's whilst I am writing. When on my return therefore to England, I first mentioned my discovery of a New Island, connected too with continents of an immense extent, I was immediately asked, in a mixed tone of confidence and derision, in what latitudes and longitudes they were all placed?—If I had answered at once, without preface or explanation, that they were in *no* latitudes or longitudes, being as I conceived no parts of the earth's surface, I admit that I might have been fairly set down as a lunatic or an impostor; because truth, when it breaks in too suddenly, con-

founds

founds the understanding, as vision is overpowered by a sudden burst of light. I thought it best therefore for the moment to practise an evasion, and answered, as indeed the truth was, that I had been obliged to comfit myself to the waves from a sinking vessel; that there being more brass than wood on my quadrant, I could not venture to use it as a raft to save me; and that if I had hung my time-piece round my neck, I should from its weight have only discovered the longitude of the bottom. Well, then, said a profound philosopher, waving for the present all localities, let us know something at least of this famous Terra Incognita.—No, Sir, I replied, you will soon, I believe, be looking for it through your telescope. I resolved, in short, to shut myself up in silence until I addressed myself, as I now do, to the whole public of this great country, and through that public to the whole civilized world.

B 2   CHAP-

4

CHAPTER I.

In which the Author gives an Account of his outward Voyage, and Shipwreck.

I SAILED from New York on the 6th of September, 1814, in the good ship Columbia, which never returned to any part of the United States, nor, until this publication, was ever heard of in any kingdom of the world. We were bound to China by the way of New South Wales, and as our voyage for nearly three months was prosperous and without unusual accident, I pass it by altogether.—On the 10th of February a storm arose, which soon increasing to a hurricane, accompanied with the most tremendous thunder and lightning, our ship, by the pressure of the one and the stroke of the other, became in a few hours an unmanageable wreck; her rudder being torn away, and her masts levelled with the decks. For nearly a month from that period a journal would be dismal and

and uninteresting, as we drifted with every change of wind or current over a trackless ocean; except that, astronomy having been rather a passion than a study from my earliest youth, I carefully noted every day at noon, by my quadrant and time-piece, our forlorn position; a precaution which I shall always consider as the most fortunate circumstance of my life. The particulars, however, are omitted; a seaman's log-book would, I suppose, have but an indifferent sale in Bond-street.

On the 16th of March, after full day had risen upon us, we found ourselves as it were overtaken by a second night.—The sea was convulsed into whirlpools all around us, by the obstruction of innumerable rocks, and we were soon afterwards hurried on by a current, in no way resembling any which navigators have recorded. We felt its influence under the shadow of a dark cloud, between two tremendous precipices overhanging and seemingly almost closing up the entrance which received us. Its im-

impetuosity was three times greater, at the least, than even the Rapids above the American Niagara; so that nothing but its almost incredible smoothness could have prevented our ship, though of five hundred tons burthen, from being swept by it under water, as our velocity could not be less, at the lowest computation, than twenty-five or rather thirty miles an hour. The stream appeared evidently to owe its rapidity to compression, though not wholly to the compression of land, its boundary on one side, if boundary it ought to be called, appearing rather like Chaos and Old Night; and what was most striking and extraordinary, we could see from the deck, not above two ships' length from us, another current running with equal force in the opposite direction, but separated from our's by pointed rocks, which appeared all along above the surface, with breakers dashing over them: Neither of the channels, as far as my eye could estimate their extent, were above fifty yards wide, nor at a greater distance from each other, and they were so even in their directions, that we

we went forward like an arrow from a bow, without the smallest deviation towards the rocks on one side, or the dreary obscurity on the other.

In this manner we were carried on, without the smallest traceable variation, till the 18th of June, a period of three months and two days, in which time, if my above-stated calculation of our progress be any thing like correct, and I am sure I do not over-rate it, we must have gone straight onward above seventy thousand miles, a space nearly three times the circumference of the earth. On the evening of that day which was to become memorable by the triumphant termination of the immortal battle of Waterloo, and which on my account also, though without any merit of mine, will be a new era in the history of the world, we found ourselves suddenly emerging into a wide sea as smooth as glass—the heavens above twinkling with stars, some of which I had never seen before, and some of our own constellations, which were visible, shone out with increased lustre, though still

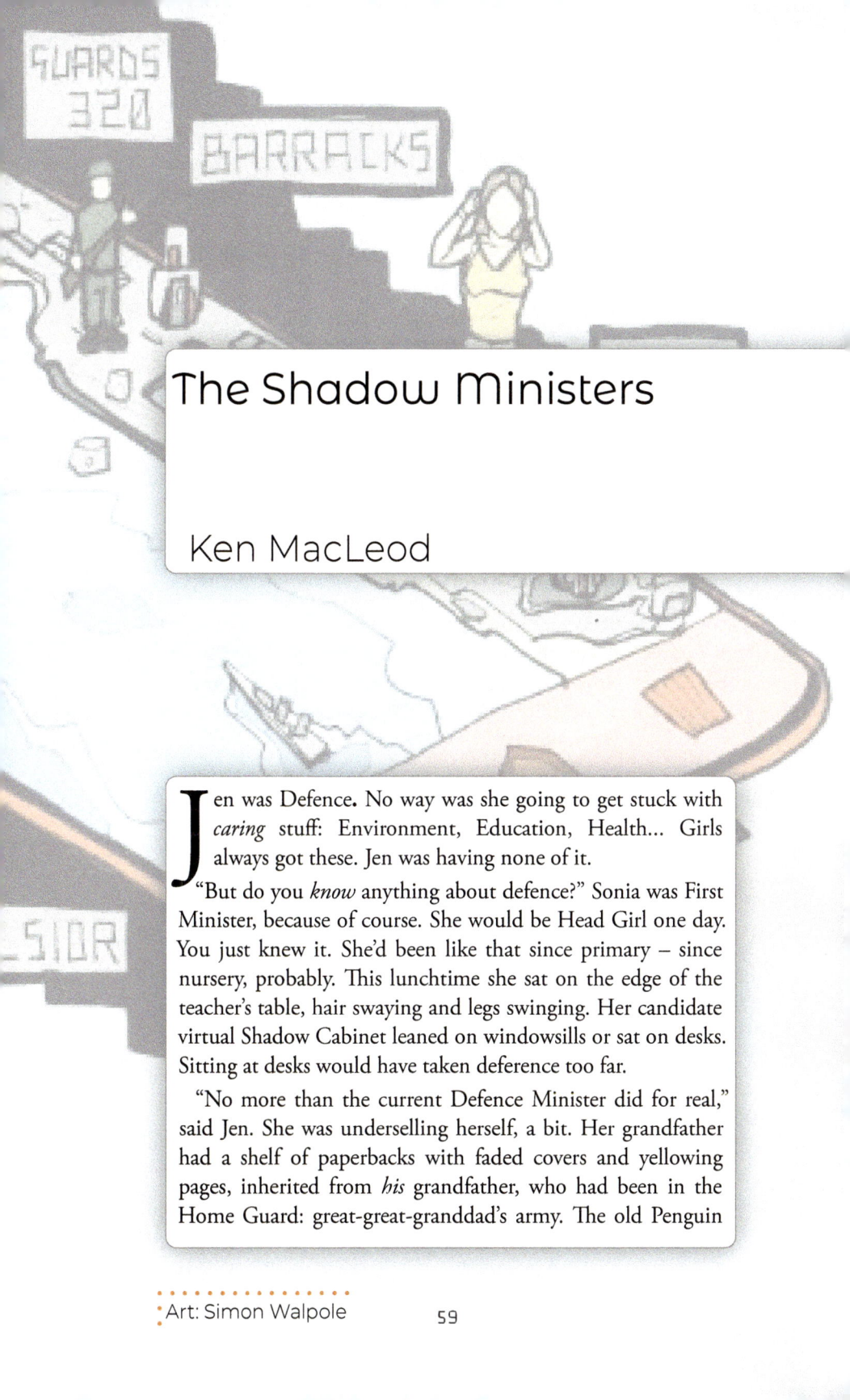

The Shadow Ministers

Ken MacLeod

J en was Defence. No way was she going to get stuck with *caring* stuff: Environment, Education, Health... Girls always got these. Jen was having none of it.

"But do you *know* anything about defence?" Sonia was First Minister, because of course. She would be Head Girl one day. You just knew it. She'd been like that since primary – since nursery, probably. This lunchtime she sat on the edge of the teacher's table, hair swaying and legs swinging. Her candidate virtual Shadow Cabinet leaned on windowsills or sat on desks. Sitting at desks would have taken deference too far.

"No more than the current Defence Minister did for real," said Jen. She was underselling herself, a bit. Her grandfather had a shelf of paperbacks with faded covers and yellowing pages, inherited from *his* grandfather, who had been in the Home Guard: great-great-granddad's army. The old Penguin

Specials had tactical suggestions. The principles were sound, the details out of date. Where now could you get petrol, or glass bottles? Jen knew better than to ask Smart-Alec. Still, there was plenty of open source material.

"I can pick it up from background. Learn on the job, like Sajid Anwar did. That's the whole idea."

Sonia pretended to give it thought. "Yeah OK,"she said. She ticked the box and moved on: "Mal? I'm thinking Energy for you?"

He looked pleased. "Aye, fine, thanks."

"Morag: Info and Comms..."

It was a Fourth Year project. The Government worried about the young: mood swings between sulking and trashing, around the baseline of having lived through the Exchanges. Live on television, even a limited nuclear war could generation-gap adolescents, studies showed. Rising seas deepened radicalisation. Civic and Democratic Engagement education challenged school students to govern a virtual Scotland, using real-time data, and economic and climate models wrapped in strategy software. The authorities burned through ten IT consultancies and tens of millions of euros before a Dundee games company offered them an above-spec product for free: SimScot.

Oak Mall connected Greenock's decrepit high street to its desolate civic square. In the years after the Exchanges it flourished, literally: hanging baskets beneath every skylight, moss shelving on every wall, planters every few metres. When the floor flooded, the mall's own carbon budget couldn't be blamed.

Two days into the SimScot project. Sonia, Jen, Mal, Jase, Dani, Morag and a couple of others walked down the hill to the mall after school and mooched along to the Copper Kettle. Cruise ships arrived weekly on the Clyde like space habitats from a more advanced culture. Today the *Star of Da Nang* was docked at Ocean Terminal, a few hundred metres away. Masked, rain-caped and rucksack-laden, Vietnamese tourists ambled in huddles, glanced at display windows in puzzled disdain and bought sweets and souvenirs at pop-up stalls. The humid walkway air was itchy with midges. The cafe had aircon and LED overheads and polished copper counters and tabletops.

"Temptation's to treat it as a bit of a skive," said Sonia. She drew on her soya shake, lips pursing around a paper straw. "Check the grading, and think again."

Everyone nodded solemnly. "Still feels like a waste of time," said Jase. He had plukes and pens.

"You're Education," Sonia pointed out. "Make me a case for dropping the requirement."

Jase looked as if he hadn't thought of that, and made a note.

"It's like having to come up with answers to your dad's questions," said Mal. He put on a jeering voice: "*What would you do instead? Where's the money going to come from? Yes, but what would you put in its place?*"

Jen laughed in recognition.

"Whit wid ye dae?" said Morag.

"Build a nuclear power station at Port Glasgow," said Mal. He gestured at the tourists outside. "Make a fortune recharging cruise ships."

Sonia flicked aside a blond strand. "Make me a case."

"No Port Glasgow though," said Morag. The town was adjacent to and even more post-industrial than Greenock. She was from there and kind of chippy about it. She considered options upriver. "Maybe Langbank?"

"Speaking of nuclear," said Jen, "I'd start by taking back Faslane, subs and all, and then annexe the North of England as far as Sellafield."

"Well," said Sonia in a judicious tone, "it could be popular..."

They all laughed. The English naval enclave across the Clyde from Greenock was a sore point.

"But not feasible," Sonia went on. "For one thing, breaking international law breaks the rules and gets you marked down. Like I said, Jen, what I want from you is exactly what the brief asks for: an independent non-nuclear defence policy."

"I thought we had one already," said Javid.

Jen had been doing her homework.

"Yes," she said, "if being small and defenceless is a policy."

"Who're we defending against?" Jase demanded.

"Well," said Jen, "that's the big question..."

"Not for you, it isn't," said Sonia. "Javid's the Foreign Secretary."

They bickered and bantered for a bit. Jen complained about toy data, and any real research getting you on terror watch-lists. Morag muttered something about a workaround for that. She picked a moment Sonia wasn't looking and slid an app across the table from her phone to Jen's.

A few minutes later Jen's phone chimed.

"Home for dinner," she said. "See you tomorrow, guys."

Morag winked. "Take care."

Jen walked briskly up a long upward-sloping street of semi-detached houses. In one of them, at the far end, her family and five other households lived more or less on top of each other. Postwar, fast-build housing had been promised. The gaps in the streets showed the state of delivery.

A male stranger's deep voice just behind her shoulder said: "Hi Jen, would you like to talk?"

"Fuck off, creep."

She leapt forward and spun around, shoulder bag in both hands and ready to shove. No one was within three metres of her. She smiled off glances from others in the homeward-hurrying crowd.

"Sorry, Jen," said a woman's voice, behind her shoulder. "I'm still getting used to this."

Again no one there.

"Stop doing that!"

"Doing what?"

"Talking from behind me."

"Sorry, again." The voice shifted, so that it seemed to come from alongside her. "It's an aural illusion. Your phone's speakers enable it."

"Not a feature I've ever asked for. Smart-Alec: settings."

"Smart-Alec is inactive."

Jen took out her phone and glared at it.

"Who are you?"

"I'm the new app your friend gave you. Call me Lexie, if you like."

"OK, Lexie. Now shut the fuck up."

After dinner Jen pleaded homework and retreated to her cubicle. She slid the partition shut, cutting off sound from the living-room, and sat on her bed, back to the pillow and knees drawn up. She flipped the phone to her glasses and started poking around.

"Lexie" turned out to be an optional front-end of Iskander, which wasn't in any app store. It had much the same functions as Smart-Alec – an interface to everything, basically – but despite the clear allusion in its name it had no traceable connection with Smart-Alec's remote ancestor, Alexa. Right now, it was sitting on top of all her phone's processes, just like Smart-Alec normally did. This wasn't supposed to be possible.

She had the horrible feeling of having been pranked, or hacked. Morag didn't seem the type to pull a stunt like that. Jen had taken for granted that Morag was savvy enough not to share malware.

Jen took the glasses off and dropped her phone, watching it fall like a leaf to the duvet. She did this a few times, thinking.

"Lexie," she said at last, "can Smart-Alec hear us?"

"No," said Lexie.

"What are you?"

"A user interface."

Jen muttered *bloody stupid literal* – "An interface to what? What is Iskander?"

"Iskander is an Anticipatory Algorithmic Artificial Intelligence, colloquially called a Triple-AI."

"How's that different from Smart-Alec?"

"This app has different security protocols. Also, Smart-Alec can give you what you ask, and suggest what else you might want. Iskander can *anticipate* what you will want."

Jen put her glasses back on, and poked some more. The app's source was listed, in tiny font on a deep page, as the European Committee. That sounded official.

"OK," she said, somewhat reassured, "show me what you can do. Anticipate me."

A map of Scotland unfolded in front of her. Ordnance Survey standard: satellite and aerial views, some of them real-time, overlaid with contour lines, names, symbols, labels...

Then as her gaze moved, the map highlighted all the military bases and hardware deployed in and around Scotland. Whenever her glance settled on a site, the display drilled down to details: personnel, weapons, fortifications, security procedures and on and on. She closed her eyes and swatted it away.

"I shouldn't be seeing this!"

"You wanted information on which to base an independent non-nuclear defence policy," said Lexie, frostily. "As you'll have gathered already, no such policy exists. Scotland is a staging area and forward base for the Alliance. The Scottish defence forces – land, sea, and air – are nothing but its auxiliaries and security guards."

Jen had always suspected as much, and had heard or read it often enough. What she'd just seen gave chapter and verse, parts list and diagrams.

"You don't have to refer to this specifically to produce a much more comprehensive and realistic policy than you could from public information," Lexie went on.

"Fuck off," said Jen.

She tried to delete the app, but couldn't. This too wasn't supposed to be possible. Smart-Alec came back to the top. The classified information vanished. Iskander still lurked, to all appearances inactive – it didn't even show in Settings – but ineradicably there, a bright evil spark like an alpha emitter in a lung.

Between classes the following morning, Jen passed Morag in the corridor. "Fight corner," she said. "Half twelve."

Morag didn't look surprised.

Between the science block and the recycle bins, a few square metres were by accident or design outside camera coverage. It was where you went for fights and other rule-breaking activities. At

12:30 Jen found a couple of Juniors snogging and a Sixth Year pointedly ignoring them while taking a puff. All three fled her glower. Morag strolled up a minute later. They faced off. Morag was stocky. She walked, and carried her shoulders and elbows, like a boy looking for trouble. As far as Jen knew, this manner had so far kept Morag out of any. She had weight and strength; Jen had height and reach. She'd done martial arts in PE. Morag played rugby.

Mutual assured deterrence it was, then.

" Whit's yir problem, Jen?"

"What the fuck d'you think you're playing at?" Jen demanded in a loud whisper. "Oh, don't give me that innocent face! You know fine well what I mean."

"You did ask. Kind ae."

"I did no such thing. How could I? I had no idea. Where did you get it, anyway?"

"Friend ae a friend," said Morag, glancing aside with blatant evasiveness. She grinned. "Had it for a while, mind. It's great! It's like a cheat code to everything."

"Yeah, I'll bet. Meanwhile you've turned me into a spy and a hacker."

"No if you don't tell anyone. I sure won't."

"Christ! What about inspections?"

Morag laughed. "It knows when to hide."

Jen scoffed. "Does it, aye?"

"I should know," Morag said, smugly. "I'm Information."

"Is that how you got it? Researching information policy?"

"No exactly. Never you mind how I got it." She spread her hands. "Come on, it's all over Europe. It was bound to turn up here eventually."

"Sounds like a new virus or a new drug."

"It's kind ae both."

"And who's spreading it? Who started it?"

Morag shrugged. "The Russians?"

"We should report this."

"What good would that do? It's still out there. The cops know about it already."

"We should report it to the school, then. It could land us in big trouble if we don't. "

"You're the Defence Minister," Morag jeered, "and you go crying you've been cyber-attacked by the Russians? No a good look, is it?"

"Not as bad as the Information Minister spreading it."

"Don't you fucking dare."

"Dare what?"

"Tell on me."

"That's not—"

"Better fucking not." In each other's faces, now.

Someone shouted "Girl fight!" People gathered. Jen and Morag stepped back.

"But if you pull a stunt like that again," Jen swore as they parted, "I'll have you."

She considered it, even as Morag swaggered away. Jen had never been so angry at anyone. She could turn Morag in, report the matter to the Police, just fucking *shop* the bitch and serve her right.

"You don't want to do that," Iskander murmured, uncannily in her ear. "You don't know what else they might find on your phone."

Jen stood stock still and stared out across the rooftops and parks to the Firth of Clyde and the hills beyond. A destroyer's scalpel prow cut the waves towards Faslane. Kilometres away in the sky a helicopter throbbed. The *Star of Da Nang* floated majestically downriver, red flag flying. Smoke from Siberia greyed the sky.

"Don't threaten me with leaving filth on my phone," she mouthed.

"Oh, I can do worse than that," Lexie said. "What you've already seen is enough to get you extradited to England, or even the US."

"You'd turn me over to the fash?"

"If you were to betray your friend – yes, in a heartbeat."

A bell rang. Jen slipped into the flow towards class, trying not to shake.

"On the bright side," Lexie added, "your friend is right. You now have a cheat code to everything. Try me."

Jen didn't consult the illicit map again. What she'd seen was enough. She set to work devising an independent, non-nuclear defence policy for a country that was already occupied. She'd joked about taking back Faslane, but the trick would be to scrupulously respect the nuclear enclave and the other bases. They would just have to be by-passed, while everywhere else was secured.

"Wait," said Sonia, when she looked over Jen's first draft of a briefing paper. "Is this a plan for territorial defence, or for an uprising?"

"They're kind of the same thing," Jen said.

"I see you've put our national defence HQ right up against the Faslane perimeter fence."

"Yup," said Jen. "Deterrence on the cheap."

"I like your thinking." Sonia flicked the paper back to Jen's phone. "Carry on."

Morag's Information policy presumed that the citizen had absolute power over what was on their phones, and that the state had absolute power to break up information monopolies. Jase on Education, and Dani on Health were likewise radical and surprising. Altogether, Sonia's team got a good grade and a commendation.

Five years later they were still a clique. They met now and then to catch up.

Jen sprinted across Clyde Square, rain rattling her hood, and pushed through swing doors under the sputtering blue neon sign of the Reserve. Mackintosh tribute panels in coloured Perspex sloshed shut behind her. Above the central Nouveau Modern bar, suspended LED lattices sketched phantom chandeliers. Drops glittered as she shook her cape dry. She stuffed it in her shoulder bag, fingered out her phone and stepped to the bar. The gang were around the big corner table. She combined a scan with a wave. Two drinks requests tabbed her glance. She ordered, and took three drinks over.

Skirts and frocks that summer were floral-printed, long and floaty or short and flirty. Jen that evening had dressed for results: black plastic Docs, silver jeans like a chrome finish from ankle to hip, iridescent navy top that quivered as she breathed. Mal couldn't keep his eyes on her. Jen smiled around and lowered the drinks: East Coast IPA for Mal, G&T for Morag, and an Arran Blonde for herself. Sonia, elegant in long and floaty, sipped green liquid from a bulb through a slender glass coil.

"It's called Bride of Frankenstein," she explained. "Absinthe and crème de menthe, mostly." Jen mimed a shudder.

Sonia's fair hair was still as long, but wavy now, or perhaps no longer straightened.

"Here tae us," said Morag, as glasses and bottles clinked. She looked around. "Bit of a step up from the Kettled Copper, eh?"

They all laughed, like the high-school climate-demo veterans they weren't.

"Coke and five straws, please, miss," said Mal, in a wheedling voice.

"Oh come *on*," said Morag. "We never did coke, even to share."

"Aye," said Jase, "we snorted powdered glass and thought ourselves lucky."

"*Powdered* glass?" Mal guffawed. "Luxury! In my day—"

"Guys," Jen broke in, "*don't* fucking start that again."

Jase leaned back, making wiping motions. "It's dead," he agreed. He'd lost his plukes but kept his nerdhood. Two pens in his shirt pocket, even on a night out.

"It has ceased to be," Mal added solemnly.

Jen shot him a warning glance. He looked hard at his pint. Conversation moved on. People changed positions on the long benches. Jen chatted with Mal for a bit, then Dani, then Morag, then Javid. She zoned out, and checked the virtual scene. In her glasses, ghosts moved through the crowd in the Reserve, collecting cash for the Committees. The closest of Greenock's Committees squatted an empty shop in the mall. Some people flicked money from their phones into virtual plastic buckets; others turned their backs. Jen waved away the phantom youth who approached her, then returned to the real world, where Morag was setting down a bottle in front of her.

"Thanks," she said, eyeing Morag as she sat down beside her. Morag raised her third G&T. "Cheers."

"Cheers. So ... how's the revolution coming along?"

"The revolution?" Morag shook her head, put her glasses on and took them off. "Oh! The Committees? Fucked if I know, hen. I got nothing to do with them."

"Oh come on."

"Seriously, Jen. Like a robotics apprenticeship would leave me time for any of that! I mean don't get me wrong, France is on strike and Germany is on fire, and we all know things can't go on like this, so good luck to these guys, but what they do is full on and a heavy gig."

"They have sympathisers."

Morag shrugged one shoulder. "No doubt. But not me."

"So what changed?"

"What do you mean?"

"You remember back at school, that SimScot thing?"

"Aye, vaguely. Load a shite. Set me firm for robotics, mind."

"You slipped me a dodgy app, remember? Called itself Iskander, or Lexie."

"Oh, aye – you were going on about wanting to research military stuff without leaving tracks, wasn't that it?" Morag laughed. "We nearly fell out over it."

"Well, yeah, when I found it was showing me actual military secrets."

"It did?" Morag's eyes widened. "All I got was business secrets!"

"There you go," Jen said. "Anti-capitalist malware."

"Do you still have it?"

"I suppose so. I could never get rid of it."

"But you don't use it?"

"Fuck, no! Anyone who does gets flagged."

"Ah, right." Morag sipped her G&T. "You're in that line now, right?"

"IT security. Yes."

"Private?"

Jen shrugged. "What is, these days? We get government contracts. Among others."

"O ... K," Morag said, voice steady as a gyroscope. "So why are you asking me about something we did when we were kids?"

"Contact tracing," Jen said. "We know where the app originated. 'The European Committee'! Talk about hiding in plain sight! We know how far it's spread, along with ... well, the attitude that it incites. But when I look back over the records it seems that you and I were, well, pretty much Patient Zero as far as Scotland's concerned. So the question of where you got it from is exercising some minds, let's say. And for old times' sake, Morag, I'd much rather you told me than that you ... had to tell someone else."

"Like that, is it?"

"I'm sorry, but yeah."

"Aw right." Morag put down her glass and spread her hands, palms up, on the table. "Honest to God, Jen, I cannae remember. I was a bad girl." Her cheek twitched. "Under-age drinking, under-age everything. Guys off cruise ships. Guys *on* cruise ships. I even went over to—" she jerked her thumb, indicating the other side of the Clyde "—what's legally England once or twice."

"Fuck sake, girl."

"You could say that."

"So *anyway*," said Morag, audibly moving on, "I was damn lucky a dodgy app was the worst I picked up."

"I'm glad," Jen said. She grinned at Morag and raised her bottle, then drank. "I am so fucking relieved you've cleared that up for me."

"Cleared it up, maybe," said Morag, grudgingly, as if not appreciating how nasty a hook she was off. "Can't say I've narrowed it down."

"Oh, that's all right. It'll give my clients something to work on. That's all they want."

What Morag had told her was what she would tell them. Jen didn't care if it was true or not. It got her off the hook, too.

Morag drained her glass. Jen stood up. "Same again?"

"Thanks."

When she got back Morag was on the other side of the table chatting to Javid, and where Morag had been Sonia was sitting. Jen set down her own drink and looked at Sonia's mad-scientist apparatus. The green liquid was almost gone.

"Can I—?" Jen ventured.

Head turned, hair tumbling. "Oh, thanks!"

"Another of these?"

"Christ, no!" Sonia laughed. "I wouldn't dare." She glanced sideways. "I see you like your Arran Blonde. I'll try one."

Jen returned with a second bottle. She hesitated, then plunged.

"Well, here's to blonde."

"Here's to—" Sonia looked puzzled.

Jen laughed. "Polychromatic."

Sonia was in Education, whatever that meant. She'd studied and now taught at the West of Scotland University. Very much a Head Girl thing, in a way, still. It was odd to see her swigging from a bottle.

"I couldn't help overhearing what you said to Morag." Apparently they'd got the catching up out of the way. "You were wrong."

"About what?"

"It isn't the Iskander app that's radicalising kids."

That sounded like quite a lot of overhearing. "Yeah? So what is it?"

"Apart from—?" Sonia made the helpless gesture, somewhere between a shrug and a wave of the hands, that meant *all this*. Flowery flutter around her forearms.

"Uh-huh."

"I'll tell you a secret." Sonia shifted closer on the bench, dress whispering. "It's the Civic and Democratic Engagement programme. The whole idea was – well, you know what it was. It backfired, but Education think that's because something isn't quite getting across. The problem is, it is getting across! They're still doing it, wondering why every year the kids come up with more and more outrageous ideas. They keep tweaking it, but nothing works."

Jen rocked back. "You mean it's SimScot?"

"No," said Sonia. "It isn't SimScot. It's just that the whole thing of pushing teenagers to think in terms of practical policies does exactly that. Like the defence policy you came up with. Or Morag's information policy: the way the problem is posed, any answer has to be revolutionary. This keeps happening." She let her eyelids drop. "I see what you're thinking, Jen. Tomorrow you'll be telling someone to dig into that games company in Dundee." Sonia's laugh pealed. "As if!"

It is SimScot, Jen thought. She was certain of it. In the morning she would—

"I've done the research," Sonia said. "Real research, I mean. Peer-reviewed and published. It's the programme, not the programme, ha-ha!"

"Have you told Education?"

"Of course I've told them. They know. They listen. They take my findings seriously. And they keep doing the same thing!" She thumped the table. "And that! Is! The Entire! Fucking! Problem!"

People were looking.

"Sorry," said Sonia. Her voice lowered. "Bit squiffy."

"Blame the Bride of Frankenstein."

"Better have some more Arran Blonde, in that case." Sonia swigged. "Another?"

They had another. It didn't help.

"Take me home," Sonia said.

Sonia lived in a high flat, looking east from Greenock. As the room brightened, Jen sat sharply up from a sleepy huddle.

"What is it?" Sonia mumbled, into the pillow.

"Something just dawned on me."

"Oh, very good," Sonia chuckled. "What?"

Jen gazed down at the cascade of yellow hair.

"It's you," she said. "It was always you. It was you all along."

"Aw," Sonia said. "That's so nice." The skin over her shoulder blade moved. Her hand brushed Jen's hip, then slipped off.

"No," said Jen. "That isn't what I—"

But Sonia had already gone back to sleep.

Jen waited for Sonia's breathing to become even, then rolled out of bed and padded over to the window. The wind had shifted, pushing the overnight rain back to the Atlantic. Smoke from forest fires in Germany hazed the rising sun. The sky above Port Glasgow was the colour of a hotplate, turned to a high level.

Ken MacLeod was born on the Isle of Lewis and now lives in Gourock on the Firth of Clyde. He has degrees in biological sciences, worked in IT, and is now a full-time writer.

He is the author of twenty novels, from *The Star Fraction* (1995) to *Beyond the Light Horizon* (May 2024) and many articles and short stories.

He has taught science fiction writing at Arvon, Moniack Mhor, and Clarion West, and was a Guest of Honour at the Glasgow 2024 Worldcon.

The Shadow Ministers was first published in Shoreline of Infinity 31, 2022

Captain Kirk visits Edinburgh in August

Rachel Plummer

He beams himself up
town to where it's busiest.
The people of this planet like to congregate
in places of religious significance
such as bus stops, overpriced kebab shops,
or around a man dressed like Yoda.

He notes it all down in his log.

Visits a hydroponics facility
known as "The Meadows"
which grows students from seed
in some hidden glasshouse.
Upon maturity, the students
are each given a single disposable barbecue
and transplanted carefully outdoors
on the first warm day of summer.

It's lonely being an away-team of one
in a city so crowded.

Kirk registers for a poetry slam under the name Tiberius,
though he can feel the old Directive
primed to take him out.
He recites some of the secret queer love
poetry he's been working on.
A lot of things rhyme with Spock.

He doesn't win
and one of the judges tells him
he needs to work on his poet-voice
which is "stilted" and "a bit too Shatner."

This planet doesn't deserve him.

He reminds himself that he could obliterate the entire city
with one well timed photon torpedo

and considers this option more seriously
after seeing his third political stand up show
and an experimental play about how smartphones are bad.

The people of this planet ebb and wane
like tides through nightful streets where light
is rockpooled under streetlamps
and each one of them is alien.

Kirk doesn't know how to phrase this for his report.

He goes back to the two-bed airbnb he's sharing with five other
    people
and thinks of his time at the Academy -
the dorms, the impossible tests, the performative nature of it all,
how for every ten of them trying to make it
only one would succeed.

He writes *Captain's Log, Stardate 23.16. I've been. I've seen*
the Fringe and all it has to show: the shows, the blows, the highs
    and lows
and this is what I've come to know:

Whatever you're looking for, it's not here.

Three stars ***

Rachel Plummer is a recipient of the
Scottish Book Trust's New Writers Award
for poetry, and has had work published
in a range of journals and anthologies.
Their first book, Wain, is a collection of
LGBTQ+ retellings of Scottish folklore.
Their latest poetry collection, *Once I*
Carried Three Crows, is published by Tapsalteerie.
Rachel lives in Edinburgh with their two children, three
guinea pigs, and entirely too many books.

O Sole Mio

Katie McIvor

What kind of ice cream van, Beth asked herself, comes round in the middle of winter?

She was washing dishes with intense noiselessness – Rory was having a blessed nap in the other room – and at the sound of the bell-like jingle she paused, confused. Her first thought was that the noise might wake Rory, and her second, how strange it was that the noise should exist at all. She wandered through the house with soapy hands, peeked gingerly over at Rory (still asleep, thank God, thank God) and stood looking out of the window. The ice cream van jingled along to the end of the road and stopped. It was January. There was nobody there, nobody outside. For a while it hunkered by the pavement, in silence. She wasn't sure how long she stood watching it; time had become meaningless in the few weeks or months since Rory's birth. The van started up again, turned in the cul-de-sac, and drove off back towards the main road, trailing its jangling music behind it.

She looked down and found she had dripped soap suds all over the pile of unopened letters on the windowsill.

Dan came home from work at half past six every evening, and that was several hours too late, really. In the few short, precious moments while Rory slept, she did her best to clean and straighten up the house, but things around her were descending inexorably into squalor. It wasn't Dan's fault, either. He did what he could, helping with the cooking, emptying the dishwasher, even sometimes putting laundry away, though not in the right places, but there were only so many hours in the evening. Then he spent the night in the spare room, trying to sleep through Rory's frequent outbursts of wakefulness, and the next day he was up at seven and out the door soon after. Each morning, when Dan left, she felt a treacly knot of despair slip into her stomach. Alone, she was alone with the baby, again.

Her dreams of escape were tinged with guilt. A good mother would treasure these days. She wouldn't wish to leave, to switch places with Dan, to hand Rory off to some imagined nanny, or just leave him lying on the floor, naked and bawling, close the door behind her, and go for a walk.

She wandered the house with Rory bouncing on her hip, singing to him, reciting half-remembered nursery rhymes. She sat on the floor and let him chew her fingers with his bone-hard gums. She tickled his chunky chins. She rocked him exhaustedly on the edge of the armchair while he screamed. She lay with him nestled on her chest, the only place he would deign to sleep for more than ten minutes at a time. While he slept she stared up at the ceiling and marvelled at the blankness inside her mind.

One day – she wasn't sure how many days had passed since the first time – she heard the ice cream van again. She was feeding Rory. Calming baby-music played in the background, and the dissonant chime of the ice cream van cut through it nauseatingly. She looked out of the window and saw the van. It was moving fast, like before, rolling purposefully past her house and along to the end of the street, where it stopped in the same place and waited. Waited for what? There were no customers, no children racing out of gardens with chattering pocket change and excited teeth. The grey January street swallowed up the bright blues and yellows of the van as if it had been sunk into a pond. When the jingle played, it sounded like it was underwater.

She started listening out for it every day. The van seemed to come irregularly, although maybe it was her own perception of time that was faulty. She was never sure any more what day it was, always encountered Saturdays with a jolt of surprise – Daddy was home, all day, which meant she could leave Rory with him and have a shower and wash her hair! – and she only ever had the vaguest idea what time of day it was. But the gurgling chimes cut through to her, wherever she was in the house. The routine from that point was unwavering: the van drove to the end of the cul-de-sac, waited for ten minutes or so in the grey doom of the council estate, and then turned and drove away. She watched it from various windows.

With Rory asleep on her chest one afternoon, she searched for clues on her phone. *Ice cream van Scotland. Ice cream van UK winter.* She couldn't have said why she was doing this; it seemed more than idle curiosity, but the nature of her interest in the van eluded her. Something about its irregular routine, she supposed, or its spontaneity – the way it could just turn round and drive out of the estate at will – had attracted her attention.

Here in her own country, she was surprised to learn, there were two types of ice cream van: a *hard van*, and a *soft van*. In her mushed-brain exhaustion she stared at this latter term for a long moment, picturing a pillowy, cushioned construction, like the walls of a soft-play area, or perhaps a whole corrugated van made out of fluted, billowing Mr Whippy. A *hard van* was armed only with a freezer, while a *soft van* packed also a special 'whippy-machine', which produced that sickly, aerated foam she remembered from childhood. To construct the ice cream van, apparently, they cut up a Ford Transit and stuck a fibreglass box on the back. She was a little disappointed by this. She had always assumed the existence of a dedicated factory from which ice cream vans were churned out fully formed, giggling their jingles in the showroom to the aproned Italian men who would drive them.

She read on. In winter, on account of the climate, it was unprofitable to run an ice cream van in the UK. Vendors had to paw in what they could during the summer heatwave, then diversify in colder months into crisps, chips, and hot dogs. The arrival of the ice cream van was signalled by the distinctive music-box jingle, or 'chimes'. British ice cream vans played a variety of popular chimes, including *Greensleeves*, *Match of the Day*, and *O Sole Mio*, the Cornetto song. A section headed 'Controversies' detailed a bitter legislative dispute over the decibel volume and permitted duration of chimes, particularly near schools, churches, and hospitals.

Rory woke with a scream that pierced her right to the fillings. She groaned upright, dropping her phone down the side of the sofa, knowing even in the moment that she would forget and search the house for it later, and set off on her incessant perambulation of the living room, the kitchen, the hallway, Rory wailing in her arms, her pulse thudding like an engine.

The following day, she was prepared. She had cleared her schedule, such as it was – washing machine emptied, breakfast plates cleaned and put away, Rory changed, Rory fed, cup of tea left to go cold in a forgotten room and then thrown down the sink, a cold slice of toast eaten for lunch, Rory changed again. All day the sense of anticipation had been building in her chest, energizing her, lifting her out of her usual baby-enforced lethargy.

By the time the van came, she was pacing the living room in her coat. The pockets chinked with coins harvested from Dan's dirty laundry. She lifted Rory out of his cot, wrapped the blanket round him, and squashed a red woollen hat onto his tiny head. Holding him in the crook of one arm, she took a deep breath and marched out of the house.

It felt very strange being outside. She hadn't washed her hair since – unclear when – and the cold January wind stirred greasy roots unpleasantly across her scalp. Should have worn a hat herself. Never mind. Stick to the mission. She wanted to laugh, at herself mostly, her determined stride towards an ice cream she did not want, but also at the emptiness of her street in this frowning mid-afternoon hour, when functional adults ought to have been off functioning, in offices or meetings or late lunches.

The ice cream van squatted by the kerb ahead of her.

She approached directly, along its pavement flank, where the hatch was, where the children should have been queuing for ice lollies. The hatch was closed. She gazed at it, her mind working slowly through the bright cartoon colours and slogans, the emblazoned *MRS WHIPPY* along the side. Why a Mrs? Who ever heard of a Mrs Whippy? She pursued her case to the cab of the Ford Transit, the driver's door, and looked through the window. There was nobody inside.

The aproned Italian man must be in the back, she thought. Maybe he came here to do his stock take. Feeling lightheaded at her own idiocy, she went round the back of the van and knocked on the painted door.

The door opened, and she saw herself standing inside.

The strangeness of this took a moment to percolate. Her mind was unaccustomed to moving quickly these days. She stared at the woman in the doorway of the van. It was her, no doubt about it. That was Beth McPherson. She knew her own face, her clammy unwashed hair, her tired eyes. She was even holding another Rory, wrapped identically in a blanket and a tiny red hat.

Fear trickled into her stomach. It wasn't just the impossibility of the situation, or the shock of seeing her own body from the outside (when had her eyes grown so sunken, and her forehead so lined?). It was also the way the other Beth looked at her: without the slightest trace of surprise, and even with boredom, or disdain. Was she really so uninteresting, even to herself? A faded, hopeless automaton, bled dry by motherhood, by life?

Her exhausted brain tried to swim its way towards understanding. This must be some kind of glitch, she told herself. A flaw in the universe. She was dreaming. She couldn't be in two places at once. That didn't happen, or not normally. But in the twilight zone of sleep deprivation since Rory's birth, it didn't seem so much of a stretch, really. She experienced a fleeting fantasy of how life could be if there really were two of her: one to drudge and express milk and change nappies, and one who could laze all day on the sofa or go out for a walk or even, heady notion indeed, go back to work. She almost giggled aloud.

The Beth in the doorway said, "I can't let you in."

She sounded so cross, so impatient. The skin under her eyes was bruised purplish.

She, the real Beth, said politely, "Why not?"

"Well, because I'm already in here," said the other Beth, as though it were obvious.

Beth thought about this.

"Okay then," she said after a moment. "I'll wait till you're finished."

The other Beth nodded, and closed the door.

Beth didn't move. And yet, when the door swung shut, she found herself suddenly standing on the other side of it, holding the handle as it closed.

She was inside the van.

She clutched Rory to her chest and twisted round abruptly, looking for the other Beth – too quickly; her head washed with lightness for an instant. Or perhaps the lightness was in the walls: the whitish chrome surfaces, the panels papered in cream with a pattern of dancing gingerbread men in party hats. There was nobody there. She and Rory were alone in the van.

The lights were on. The engine was running; there was power. Where was the nice man in the apron? Where was Mrs Whippy?

Where – a chill down her back – was the other Beth?

Rory made a small noise: *buh bah*. Automatically, she relaxed her knees and bobbed on the spot with him, rocking him in her arms.

To her right stood the freezer cabinet, invitingly stocked with colourful ice lollies. On the counter were large rectangular boxes of toppings. And there was the whippy-machine, just as she had read about. The long white handle which, if pulled, would send soft-serve creaming out of the nozzle.

"Look, baba," she whispered to Rory. "Here's the On button. See, on the side? And here are some nice lights on the panel. They're telling us the temperature, I think. And you can hear the ice cream churning round and round inside. Perhaps we could…"

She looked around: guiltily, the well-brought up Scottish schoolgirl, not wanting to steal. There was nobody there. She fished out some of Dan's coins and dropped them on the counter before helping herself to a cone. It was a struggle to get it out of the stack one-handed. She had to shuffle Rory into her elbow so she could hold the cone and pull the handle down at the same time. Rory watched the ice cream foam past his eyes, a gentle flumping of dairy, folding itself in a sloppy spiral into the cone. Beth held it clumsily to her lips. She felt breathless. She extended her tongue to the sweet, lingible surface, smoother-than-smooth, silky and soft as a baby's cheek.

The sensation triggers an abrupt up-wash of memory. She is six, or maybe seven. In the square patchy gardens of her street, children with change in their pockets, the endless afternoon sun on pink necks, the squall of mothers yelling over fences. The chimes which seem to come from under the sea and promise sand. How she runs, her feet bare on the baking pavement, hot coins searing her fingers. The queue, the jostle of small legs and arms. How she has to reach up over her own head to pass the money to him, aproned Italian giant in the van; how he smiles down like a near-god and hands her carefully the towering, wobbling mound in its cheap ecru cone. The insertion of tongue into foam, cold-cold, sweet-sweet, the taste of young summer.

Rory squawks, startling her; she's forgotten he is there. She gives him some ice cream. *You'll rot his teeth, you will,* complains her own mother in the back of her mind, but he doesn't have teeth yet. He likes it. His baby-eyes chuckle and wink for more.

She's not sure how long she stays in the van. She dawdles up and down, bouncing the happy baby, showing him the sprinkles and flakes, the gingerbread men on the walls. They're both children again, in her mind. He could be someone's baby brother, clamped clumsily to her hip, while outside parents look on with indulgence and take photographs. But parents don't matter here. They're in the promised land, the home of sweet treats. This is the edible house to which the little children flock. These are the ice lollies, red-orange-yellow; these the wafer cones.

A knock at the door distracts her. She opens it, impatient, knowing what she will see: herself, standing outside, cold, older, greasy-haired. She doesn't want the company. "I can't let you in," she says rudely – the blank, unthinking rudeness of childhood.

From her own pinched mouth outside: "Why not?"

"Well," she says, remembering her line and wanting to laugh suddenly, "because I'm already in here."

She doesn't listen to the other Beth's reply. She's already heard it. She closes the door, wondering if she can stomach another coneful of froth. But when the door swings shut, she finds herself somehow outside on the steps, holding the handle, pulling the door towards her, although she hasn't moved.

Dan came home and seemed to think everything was fine. He was tired, yawning into his pasta, forgetting where he'd put his car keys.

"Does it feel like this day's been twice as long as normal?" she asked him as they went to bed.

"Tell me about it," said Dan.

In his cot by the side of the bed, Rory wriggled and twisted, fretful although deeply asleep, his tiny hands balling helplessly at the air.

Time passed. At least, it did for others. Beth, strangely, no longer felt its weight. She forgot things: little things, like when she'd last emptied the washing machine, or what Dan had asked her to add to the shopping list. These omissions didn't appear to matter. The future seemed of little concern to her. She found it hard to summon much interest in Dan, either. He came home, sometimes, and said all the things he usually said, and sometimes he left, and she didn't really notice. She and Dan, she sensed, were no longer travelling in the same direction. They danced past each other, occupying the same house but at an ever-increasing distance, their lives diverging, like strangers whose paths once crossed briefly at a railway station before boarding different trains.

Beth changed, or perhaps she *unchanged*. Lines that had been deepening around her eyes disappeared. She stared for minutes on end into the mirror, while Rory bawled in his basket. She looked for grey hairs, but counted fewer and fewer of them; soon there would be none at all. Every day she felt brighter, more awake, more herself.

She took Rory to the baby group at the library. The other mothers – haggard creatures, they seemed to her now, baggy and leaking and ugly – opened their mouths and, after pausing, asked Beth what new product she'd been using. The envy in their eyes disgusted her. She was no longer like them. Their future was no longer hers.

When she got home, Dan frowned, tipped his head to one side like a dog, and asked if she'd done something to her hair. She just smiled.

It wasn't as if it was a definite decision, after all, she told herself. The ice cream van still came every day. She saw it rolling past the window, as free and unbothered as a bird, the young woman in the driver's seat with her mouth wide open, singing along to the jingle. At any point, Beth told herself, she might decide to go back out, to knock once more on the door, to undo what had been done, whatever that was. She'd tried to puzzle it out. She flicked through Dan's old physics books, reading about the time travel paradox and closed time-like curves, about free will and causal loops and predestiny. None of it quite seemed to apply to her situation. The laws of physics were unable to explain how one might close a door and find oneself, without transition, on the other side of it; how one might enter an ice cream van and prompt time to run backwards.

Even if she couldn't understand what was happening to her, she was curious to see where it would lead. Already her breasts felt drier, as if the milk were flowing in reverse; she pumped and out came air. She had to put pads in her underwear again to catch the renewed dribble of lochial blood. She watched with interest as hormonal blotches reappeared on her skin, spots which she had thought were gone, time unwriting itself on her body. And on Rory's body, too. That made sense: he was part of her, in a way that Dan was not; Rory was a piece of her own body that had become mistakenly detached.

She and Dan walked round the block, with Rory in his carrier strapped to Dan's chest. The day felt fresh and oddly warm, although it was winter. Neighbours passed by them, smiling, waving across the street at the tiny baby in his red woolly hat.

Beth waved back.

"He's been asleep the whole way round," said Dan, gazing down at Rory. "Is he okay?"

"He's fine," Beth said.

The ice cream van sailed past the road end. The driver was nodding her head to the music, tossing her hair around, free to go exactly where she chose. Free to drive all the way to the seaside, trundle her van down the beach, and vanish beneath the waves.

"An ice cream van?" Dan said. "In January?"

Beth said nothing.

At the end of the week, the health visitor came round for Rory's check-up. "He's lost weight," she said, sounding perplexed. "Unusual at this age. He looks very healthy, though. Has he been feeding normally?"

Beth smiled and nodded.

Dan was home early from work. He waited until the health visitor was gone, then cornered Beth in the kitchen, where she was trying to read an article on her phone. Rory was asleep in his arms. "Beth, love, is everything okay? What did she mean about Ro-Ro losing weight?"

"I'm sure it's normal," Beth said. "They go up and down."

"Has he been sick at all? Has anything happened to him?"

Beth peered at Dan across the kitchen. He looked different, or perhaps she just remembered him differently. At university they had gone swimming in the river together and stayed up all night watching bad films, their legs curled around each other on the narrow student mattress. She didn't understand how this greying, thin-faced man in front of her could possibly be the same person.

"Rory's fine," she said at last. "I'm fine. Stop worrying about us."

Dan reached a hand out towards her, shifting Rory's dead weight against his chest. He touched her hair. Beth was pleased with her hair today; it was no longer falling out in clumps, and it looked as glossy and shiny again as it had during pregnancy. "You do look happy," Dan said, and he was smiling, although his voice was sad.

Beth grinned back at him.

"We'll get him weighed again next week," said Dan. "It's probably nothing."

"Of course it's nothing," said Beth.

Soon she wouldn't have to worry about these things. Her body was growing, re-enlarging, staking out space within for what was coming back to her. She was looking forward to it. Things in reverse, things returning to their rightful order. Soon she would be at peace again, the weighted peace of the heavily expectant, glowing from within. No more the anxious wrench of Rory leaving her arms, leaving her sight. Soon he would be back where he belonged. She sang to herself as she walked him round and round the house, his little form lighter and smaller each day. When he cried, she shrugged and popped her headphones on. Everything became bearable, easier, with an endpoint in near sight.

And after that endpoint, maybe, she would keep going. Back and back she could go, into her own youth, to childhood: the feel again of the foamy soft-serve licking her tongue, the tug of excitement in her guts at the sound of the ice cream van's chimes.

Rory slept more and more as his skull shrank. She massaged her augmenting abdomen and dreamed of the day when he would sleep once more inside her, returned to his original state, purpled and slimed, abortively small, smothered away deep within her flesh.

Katie McIvor is a Scottish writer. She studied at the University of Cambridge and now lives in the Scottish Borders with her husband and daughter. Her short fiction has appeared in magazines such as The *Deadlands, Uncharted,* and *Little Blue Marble.* You can find her on Twitter at @_McKatie_ or on her website at katiemcivor.com.

O Sole Mio was first published in Interzone 295, September 2023

What a team! Science and Science Fiction

Pippa Goldschmidt

Science short story anthologies published by Shoreline of Infinity

What do waste-eating-mushrooms, the precise colour of Mars, the science of sleep, microbial computers, rocket launching sites in the Highlands, and resurrecting the dead all have in common? They've all been the subject of short stories published in four anthologies by Shoreline of Infinity that explore the fictional potential of up-to-date science and technology here in Scotland.

Biopolis: Tales of Urban Biology, Once Upon a Biofuture - Tales For A New Millennium, A Practical Guide to the Resurrected and *Scotland in Space* contain short stories, as well as non-fiction essays by academics exploring the inspiration behind the fiction. Fiction that has taken inspiration from real science and attempted to represent it accurately without falling into the trap of the ever-treacherous and tedious 'info-dump'.

Although each anthology has been the result of a slightly different process, what they all share is a more collaborative way of producing the end results than is usually the case when a solitary writer sits down in front of their laptop or notebook. Perhaps these processes are more akin to what happens in a laboratory where teams of people, who each may have slightly different specialisms, work together to achieve a common goal. So perhaps it's worth unpacking those processes in more detail:

Futuristic visions of cities in science fiction often start with 'shiny' hard-edged technologies dominated by inorganic materials, for example metals and glass. *Biopolis: Tales of Urban Biology*, edited by Larissa Pschetz, Jane McKie, and Elise Cachat, concentrates on the life sciences, asking how future urban environments might depend on the emerging field of synthetic biology, in which organic substances are engineered to produce an impact on our environment. For this anthology writers were each matched up with scientists from the University of Edinburgh to learn about their research in areas including the use of enzymes to recover waste metals, the control of circadian rhythms, and the development of new marine biofuels. Each short story is accompanied by an explanatory paragraph written by the relevant scientist. This might be seen as the conventional approach to writing 'accurate' or hard science fiction, in which the fiction writer learns from the expert scientist.

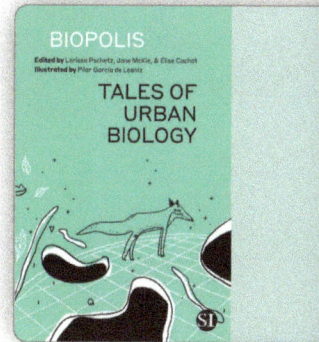

Once Upon a Biofuture: Tales for a New Millennium also takes synthetic biology as its starting point, but in contrast nearly all of the contributory pieces, including short stories, were written by scientists themselves. The anthology was edited by Jessica Fox, a former storyteller for NASA who worked as an artist-in-residence at the UK Centre for Mammalian Synthetic Biology at the University of Edinburgh where she collaborated

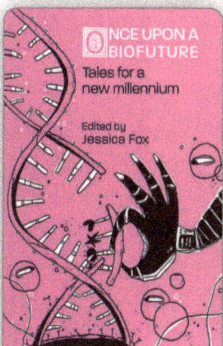

89

with the scientists to produce these pieces. Her role was necessarily more in-depth than an editorial one usually is, in that she enabled and supported the scientist-authors from beginning to end, through recording and transcribing their emerging works, as well as workshopping and editing. The process allowed the scientists to lead the storytelling and retain their creative voice while working with an experienced writer to shape the narrative. A couple of the scientists here open up on 'life in the lab' and reflect on aspects of their day-to-day professional lives and the nature of these new interdisciplinary sciences that affect how people from different disciplines communicate with each other. Two contributors have written memoirs linking the specific aspects of their childhoods (in Islay and Glenrothes, respectively) with their subsequent research careers. Other contributors have written science fiction set in the future. Perhaps synthetic biology, an interdisciplinary science that brings together researchers from different backgrounds, can learn from this inherently collaborative and interdisciplinary process.

Scotland in Space, edited by Deborah Scott and Simon Malpas, arose as part of a wider activity; the 'social dimensions of outer space' (SDOS) network which has brought together an informal group of writers, artists, and academics (mostly based in Edinburgh) interested in space exploration, focusing on Scotland both as a site for successful industrial and academic space activities, and also considering the wider social implications of those activities. The anthology was kicked off by a workshop which brought together the writers and academics to explore the pre-agreed themes of Mars exploration, exoplanets and cosmology. The book comprises three sections, in each of which a (fairly lengthy) short story is accompanied by essays that respond to the ideas the story evokes, identifying, exploring and commenting upon the physical, social and cultural possibilities and potentials evoked in the science fiction.

A Practical Guide to the Resurrected, edited by Gavin Miller and Anna McFarlane, takes as its starting point the ever-increasing advances of medical science such as genome editing, lab-grown organs and advanced bionics, and considers the medical frontier and our futures. What happens to society when the dead can be brought back to life? When big pharmaceutical companies create illnesses as well as cures? When a chip in your brain can take away depression for good?

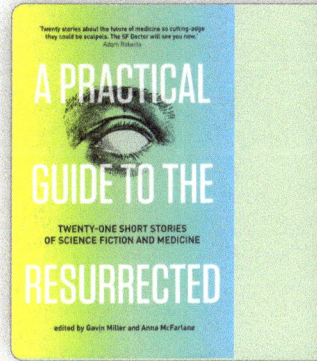

Unlike the other anthologies, the stories included in this one are the shortlisted and winning entries in a competition run by the editors from their academic home in the English Lit department at the University of Glasgow, as part of an academic project called 'Science fiction and the medical humanities' which aimed to investigate how science fiction and medicine work together in the public imagination. Medical humanities is a field that highlights the essential interdisciplinarity of medicine, and is interested in understanding how narratives of medicine (for example those told by a patient to a doctor), as well as its history and philosophy, influence medical practice and practitioners. The purpose of the competition was to find out how science fiction can tell stories of future medical breakthroughs. The editors in this case could only respond to the already-completed stories and had no role in shaping them.

The process of presenting work by fiction writers and academics side by side isn't unique to Shoreline of Infinity; over the past few years Comma Press, based in Manchester, have also been publishing the results of science-inspired stories, alongside essays

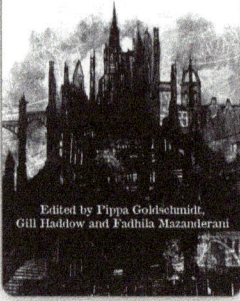

Uncanny Bodies

Edited by Pippa Goldschmidt, Gill Haddow and Fadhila Mazanderani

written by scientists, in several anthologies. Luna Press (also based in Edinburgh, like Shoreline) have published *Uncanny Bodies*, in which writers and academics used the concept of Freud's uncanny to examine our complex relationships with our own bodies, cities and landscapes.

I should now declare a personal interest, as well as co-editing *Uncanny Bodies*, I also have stories in three of the four anthologies I've discussed here. There's something about this interdisciplinary process that seems to be greater than the sum of its parts. Perhaps

its because these anthologies were all created in Scotland, a country famous for its 18th century Enlightenment in which scientists, philosophers, artists and writers communicated with each other in the coffee houses of Edinburgh to extend human knowledge and understanding. Perhaps we can see these anthologies as a modern attempt to recreate the circumstances of the Enlightenment, and break down what feels to me to be increasingly artificial barriers between literature and science.

Pippa Goldschmidt lives in Edinburgh and Berlin. She has a background in astronomy and is particularly interested in writing about science. Most recently she is the author of *Night Vision*, and co-editor of *Uncanny Bodies*.)

Her work has been broadcast on BBC Radio 4 and published in ArtReview, Tamarind, BBC Sky At Night magazine, Times Literary Supplement and Magma. Pippa is Contributing Editor (non-fiction) for SF Caledonia.

SF Caledonia – free reading

All our stories are available for free reading on the website - designed for quick access and easy reading on any device. Here's a pair for you to read via the QR code portal.

Ely Percy
The Alien Invasion

Ah wis abducted by aliens wance. Never tolt anywan but. It wis nearly forty year ago an ah knew whit folk wid say. The wans in ma class wid be aw, Did yi aye? Zat when yi had yir first anal probe? Zat why yir a fuckin space cadet? Probly widda thought ah wis jist makin it up fur attention anyway. Ma ma an da definitely wid.

That's whit they tried tae say that time ah smacked ma heid aff the livin room waw after ma da shoved me oot the road ae the telly – they tried tae say thir wis nothin up wi me, that ah wis jist pure at it, pure tryin tae get extra time aff school.

https://sfcaledonia.scot/urls/ai

Neil Williamson
Fish on Friday

Hello, Ms MacArthur? Hi, there. This is a courtesy call from ASDaTESCo. My name is—

ASDaTESCo. The Agency for Sport, Diet and Technology Empowering Scotland's Citizens. My name is Aiden—

You *know* who we are, Ms MacArthur. Our representatives have had cause to contact you several times already this year. Well, that's not very nice. We're *not* Nazis. The ASDaTESCo initiative has been instrumental in transforming this nation from the Sick Men and Women of Europe into a horde of happy, healthy Hamishes. Yes. Yes, *Hamishes.* It's from our advertising campaign. You must have seen it.

https://sfcaledonia.scot/urls/fif

Eagles

Iain Bain

Eagles was a runner-up in the Cymera Festival/ Shoreline of Infinity Scottish short story competition, 2024

Dear Humphrey

Sorry, I know, I missed another deadline. It wasn't my fault this time, honestly. It was the eagles. I meant to get my piece in on time, I was pretty sure I was going to get my piece in on time, and I would've I got my piece in on time. If it wasn't for the eagles.

You won't know what it's like at my place: it's a corridor of tenement buildings, red sandstone, like parallel cliffs facing each other, and I'm on the top floor. It's a quiet street and I've got my desk at the window, so I can look out at what's going on, watch the people coming and going and think about nothing much other than getting on with my work and what time's dinner. Till the eagles came.

Like you'd expect, there was just one at first, a big cocky bastard, he comes battering down the street, wheels up and he's standing on my window ledge looking at me like, 'What the fuck are you looking at?' 'What kind of eagle?' you'll be asking, 'like, was it a sea eagle or a white-tailed eagle or what?' Well

I'll tell you,
it was a golden
eagle, but just in case
you don't know, and I hope I'm not being
patronising here, 'cause that's the last thing in my intentions,
they're really more of a dark brown, so I don't know where they
get that name from. Just goes to show. Anyway, he's stalking
about, this big feathery prick, and I'm thinking this is all well

and good but Humphrey is expecting me to get my piece in on time and I can assure you that concentration is not enhanced with a three-foot flying killing machine, talons, flesh-ripping beak and mean-eyed stare, the whole set, just two feet away from you. There has to be some kind of, you know, development. Then it occurs to me: liquorice. You know how eagles love liquorice? It doesn't matter if you don't; it's just one of those things you know or you don't. Well, I've got a box of liquorice allsorts in the top cupboard, been there since Christmas. If I give the bird some of my liquorice allsorts, not the blue beady ones 'cause they taste like shit, maybe it'll be happy with that, move on, bother some other writer. There's a guy in Stewartsville Street does travel books, maybe he is out of liquorice and he'll get stuck with this situation. You're probably saying to yourself that's just plain selfish, but I was also thinking of you and your deadline, remember Humphrey, and anyway, I hate travel books. There's something show-offish about that stuff, don't you think? 'Marvelling at the breathtaking, lush green vistas, we gorged ourselves on the local quai-quai fruit and sipped the fermented sap of the 'nkaka trees as our rickshaw whisked us into the cobalt night...' You know? So I get out the box and they're a bit sticky, kind of gooey in places, to tell the truth, but I get a handful of the things, open up the side window, just a few inches, not wanting to lose any fingers, all of which I prize and require. Out they go, pink, white, brown, orange ones. Our golden friend gives me this look. I don't mind admitting, that with all my years and all the thousands and millions of words, beautiful, inspired, brilliant words, I've churned out over those years I cannot describe that look, but I'll tell you this: it made me feel small. I shrink a little when I think about it. This from a fucking bird, don't forget. This thing has the time to reduce me to nothing with his big eagle eyes, give something that could only have been a shrug, streak off the window ledge and pull a pink coconut wheel out of the air before it reaches the ground. If I had a favourite, and I don't, it'd probably be the coconut wheel, pink or yellow, it's all the same to me. Then I see them. Five maybe six more eagles must have spotted the liquorice or smelt it or something, I don't know. I'm no twitcher. My guy, the first eagle, makes it clear he doesn't need company and the allsorts are not for sharing. Next thing there's a dog-fight up and down White

Street. They are all skiting about the place, trying to tear lumps out of each other. Feathers flew, as they say. So did chunks of eagle meat and blood, just to give you the picture.

At this point they must have rounded a corner, cause right then Mr Parchment from number sixty-two comes out shaking his warty old fist at me, calling me a dirty bastard and what did I think I was doing throwing my rubbish onto the street. I open my window and shout back about the eagles. 'What, he says, in Partick? What are they doing here?' I tell him I don't know but then he says maybe they're making another record, which is stupid because there's no decent recording studio in Partick and, anyway, they're all retired millionaires who hate each other, aren't they? And I tell him so, even though this is precisely not the point, what with these lethal birds of prey tearing around the neighbourhood, not the Californian cowboy rock stars, but then he starts singing,' You can't hide your lyin' eyes…' and I wonder whether he's having a dig. I let it go.

Then the flight of eagles comes tearing out of Gardner Street and there's a bit of a stand-off round about the chimney stack at number seventy-four. Some roof tiles slide off and smash down there on the pavement. There would be a few folk in the even numbers getting questionable TV reception too, what with the way some of those things were twisting up the aerials. 'Countdown' would have been on about then. 'Ah,' says Mr Parchment when he finally sees the birds, 'eagles,' which is what I said in the first place. He nods and he calls across to me 'Monkeys, that's what we want,' and he turns and goes back into his close. It was like he was saying I'll get a screwdriver or a stepladder something. Funny how some people come up with answers to stuff when everyone else is just scratching their heads. I wouldn't have thought of monkeys.

I'd just popped into the kitchenette to make myself some Horlicks when this van pulls up, tooting its horn like billio. Mr Parchment comes out and he has a word with the driver, goes to the back door and pulls it open. Out they come, harum-scarum, dozens of the buggers. They're swinging on the few scraggy stunted trees in the front gardens and climbing up the drain

pipes. Before you know it some of them had reached the roof and then there's a big shouting match. I don't know if they were howler monkeys but howling was what they were doing alright, howling, screeching and chucking stones, slates, anything they could pick up, at the eagles. Do you think the birds take this lying down? No, they don't. One big fellow with a beak about the size of a shovel comes tearing down, picks up a monkey with these big fuck-off talons they've got and lets it drop to the ground in my back green. Bam! Horrible. The housing association are kind of slow on repairs and I just couldn't see cleaning up dead monkey splattered over the bin shelter as being something they're going to rush into.

This was turning into a bit of a stramash and what with the racket and everything, wouldn't you just know it, the lions arrive. I know there's a pride hangs about in Mansefield Square; I've seen them dossing about down there, yawning and eyeing up the kids playing basketball. So here they come padding down the middle of the road, swinging their shoulders, cool as the winter breeze. The eagles don't like this. They start buzzing them, taking swipes with their claws. The monkeys start on the chimney pots, chucking them down into the melee going on down there. The lions are getting pretty annoyed now. They are lazy bastards but you just don't mess with them, so they're having a go back and their claws are serious, let me tell you. Of course with lions you're going to get hangers on; it's just the way it is. Hyenas, prairie dogs, meerkats even: I hate those little fuckers, must be the adverts. Soon the street is heaving with fighting, roaring, screeching creatures. It's a bloodbath. You've never seen anything like it, Humphrey, I can assure you. Not in the West End, not on a Tuesday afternoon. I'm sure I heard an elephant. There was definitely a giraffe stuck in the close, so Mrs McClivey couldn't empty her bins. I got humming birds in my shirt. Christ, there's a swordfish in my bath. Now how the holy fuck did that get there?

I've had enough of this shit, I can tell you, so I call the council. Would you believe it, this simpleton at the other end says she can't help me with nothing till I give her a specific department she can put me through to. Well how the fuck do I know? The department of getting the screaming bloody animal Armageddon the fuck off my street. Have you got one of those Mrs? I ring the police, the fire brigade, the Daily Record, the BBC. I ring everyone I think might pay a bit of notice, or make someone who can do something about this mess pay attention. Nothing. Hours pass and so, I have to tell you, Humphrey, did your deadline. You see what I'm dealing with here? I get a cup of tea and a Kitkat and go to take another look out at the biblical disaster unfolding at my front door. The floor is shaking, there's this almighty grinding, roaring, whining sound and there's an Apache helicopter just sitting there outside my bay window. It just hangs there on the air like God's in the cockpit and its fucking judgement day. The shooting starts, rockets, machine guns, the whole bastard works. White Street turns red. You want a thing like this fixed but this was brutal. I went back to my bed and stayed there under the duvet till it finished.

When I got up this morning the laptop had run out of battery and I couldn't find the cable. There were guys in those white suits still washing down the streets. No-one was let in or out. The kids in the primary school down the road would've had to walk round by Dumbarton Road. I see Mr Parchment standing at his window shaking his head and looking old. By lunchtime there was nothing left. The military, scientific, whatever they were, have all gone. I felt like... I don't know, I just felt...desolate, sick at heart. For a long time I just stood by that window tears running down my face. Stupid.

So, yes, hands up, I am a bit late with my piece this week. Sorry. Okay? Fucking eagles.

Iain Bain has had short stories and articles published, short drama performed, and sketches, songs and a comedy-drama series broadcast by BBC Radio Scotland. He spent several years working as an editor for some of the larger UK publishers and the BBC. A former Scottish Book Trust New Writers Award winner, Iain writes and records with his band, Radio Ghosts..

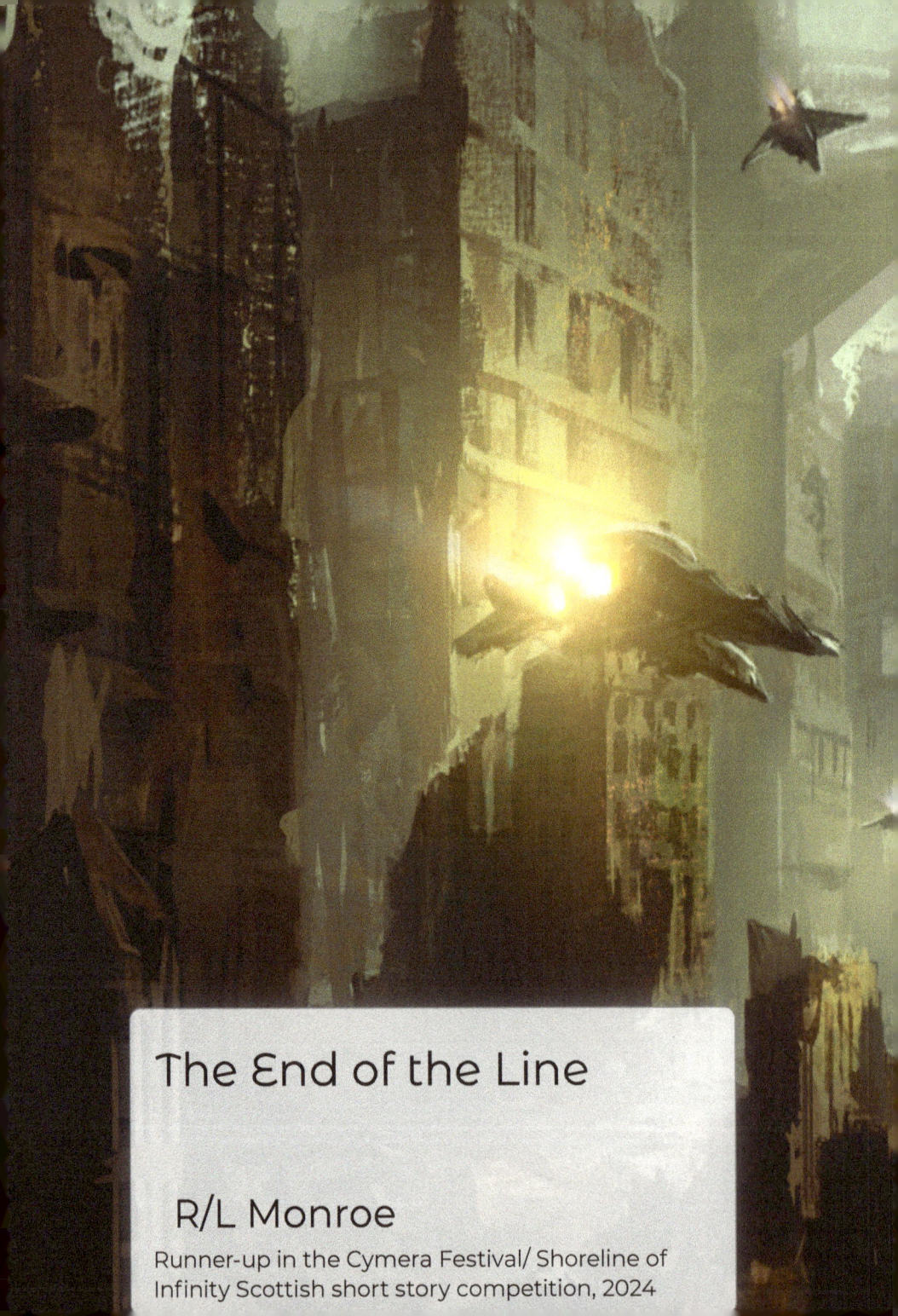

The End of the Line

R/L Monroe

Runner-up in the Cymera Festival/ Shoreline of
Infinity Scottish short story competition, 2024

Cam was working the line the day beans toppled Gilgamesh, the City Where All Rivers Met. So history records. But history has a habit of looking in the wrong direction when it matters.

Kitchen L17 was down a hand. Not in the sense that anyone was missing – Zubair's legs were shot, but they'd strapped him into a ceiling dolly so he could still whizz up and down the line. Vanya was sick but sealed into a quarantine suit, maintaining the vegetable filter whenever she wasn't retching into her collar. They were *down a hand* in that one of their section waiters cut his off.

The culprit was a faulty sensor. Tableside had complained about them for years. The waiter was securing a caddy clip when down came the vacuum tube and bit him off at the wrist. The first the kitchen knew about it was a commotion from the dishwashers when a severed hand plopped into the steam cleaner. The second was when the waiter came down the Returns chute. He'd just had the presence of mind to fold himself into the dumbwaiter before he blacked out. And that was how it began.

"Fuck me." Cam had almost shunted him straight into the garbage disposal on autopilot.

"Hands!" shouted Kalea. Dishes crowded the conveyor, waiting for QA. Cam hammered the blinking green button. *Approve. Approve. Approve.*

"Waiter down!" Cam yelled. They checked the fallen soldier's wristpad. "T19."

"You're shitting me," came Min's voice from the turnover station. Vanya's mouth moved behind her visor, but she'd got the suit with the broken radio. She quacked.

"Serious," called Cam, easing the waiter's pad off his stump. "He's punched out."

"Someone get up there. Next booking's inbound. We're already behind."

"Not it," shouted Kalea. Cam looked from Zubair's harness to Vanya gurgling in her suit.

"Fuck me," they conceded.

Nobody wanted to be Tableside. You were better off sucking clogs out of the steam cleaner. You were better off crawling under greasy conveyors in the rat run. Uniform and pay didn't matter. Cam would have given two fingers to get out of it, but a severed hand trumped them.

By the time they got to T19, a neat, blunt woman in a designer sarong was waiting in the vacuum lift. *Amika Solak* said the wristpad. Cam swiped her in, and she started up before she was even seated.

"I booked for 15:27. It's 15:29. You left me waiting *two full minutes*. Absolutely disgusting. And my meal's not here. Is *this* the standard of service you advertise?"

"No ma'am," said Cam. "Sorry. We're-"

"Excuse me, don't talk back. Where's my food?"

Her order was already in the system and cleared by QA. Cam hit *Serve* and the lethal vacuum tube swished from the ceiling and locked into the centre of her table. It fired a silver cylinder down, sighed, and retracted in a cloud of steam. Amika looked at Cam.

Tableside was a relic of an older time. It was one of the crown jewels of the Gilgamesh restaurant district. Prep, chefing, service and cleanup were all automated these days, but it was widely agreed that convenience came at the sad cost of a human touch. The man Cam stood in for wasn't really a *waiter* any more than the mechanics on the line were *cooks*, but customers enjoyed the fantasy.

Cam leaned forward and unlatched serving dishes one by one. Seasoned waiters could do it in a gesture, like a magic trick, but Cam sweated and fumbled the magnetised pins.

"Shocking," said Amika. "Disgraceful. I'm tracking the time you waste, and I will expect to be repaid."

Above all, diners missed having somebody to lambast. *They want to be heard* was the way Central put it. It was no fun being wealthy without someone to be wealthy at.

"Where are the beans?" she asked, when Cam had unfolded the full spectrum of her meal. Cam looked at the caddy, then back at her.

"Am I allowed to speak?"

"I booked the Sunday Classic With Beans. Do you see beans here?"

"No, ma'am."

"I *paid* for beans. Send it back."

What else could they do? They latched up the compartments and hit *Return*. As swiftly as it had appeared, the silver caddy shot down the dumbwaiter.

The trouble was that beans had been abolished. This could be traced to Tourist Board focus testing, years back when Gilgamesh was only *The City Where Most Rivers Meet if you Disregard Tidal Peninsulas and Count Some Minor Bits of Coastline*. It was determined that *The City Where All Rivers Meet* sounded catchier and fit better on imperial letterhead. Thus, an unprecedented – and ultimately catastrophic – geoengineering project had been undertaken.

At first it went well. The provinces dried up (and the less said about the barbarian badlands past the borders the better) but distant drought and famine brought a wealth of cheap labour to Gilgamesh. Its luxurious automated systems flourished in the care of a vast custodian workforce. Whatever settlements withered in the desert were soon replaced by hydroponic river-towns. And that was where beans came in.

The sun got hotter. Rivers dwindled, and the reservoirs of Gilgamesh filled. Crops were reprioritised. Six months before the collapse, it was decided that beans didn't make sense for the Empire. They were too thirsty, too low yield. They offered nothing that lentils or fungi couldn't replace. They were abolished.

Amika was on a flight surveying the badlands when she'd made her reservation. It was late afternoon over the western sea, but as she tapped *Confirm* it happened to be precisely midnight in Gilgamesh. That would have been fine, and the Empire should have stood for another thousand years, except the Agricultural district's computer systems considered 00:00 to be the first minute of the day, while the Kitchen district systems understood it to be the last.

One minute later, and her Sunday Classic With Beans would have been suitably truncated. Instead, she slipped between ones and zeroes and drove her wrench deep into the heart of the auto-city.

Kitchen L17 was soon in the weeds without Cam. They'd already cranked their machines to Turbo, and hauled Zubair up over the line on his dolly so he could grease and clean the works without slowing service. They'd even propped the dazed waiter at Cam's QA station, with his stump taped up in poly-wrap and a quick adrenal shot to wake him up.

He didn't bat an eye when Amika's caddy dropped into Returns. He'd served twenty Sunday Classics that day; hers looked fine to him. Picky customer. He shunted it into the garbage disposal and hit *Redeploy*.

Two blocks and one hundred miles of intricate conveyances away, the L district Fulfilment system spat an error. *Component empty*. Not *invalid order* – it was impossible to enter an invalid order, and doubly impossible for central to delegate one out to Fulfilment. Anything booked in was a valid order. Therefore, Fulfilment reasoned, L district was out of beans.

"We're out of beans," said Cam, "What about lentil puffs, or verdant mushroom crisp?"

"What did I order?" snapped Amika. "Can you read? What did I pay for?"

"Sunday Classic With Beans," said Cam "But-"

"*But?* This isn't a discussion. This is outrageous." Her voice rose over the piped-in ambience, smothering fountains and birds. "I could take you to court for breach of contract."

Cam flicked through the wristpad's smiling, useless interface. *Cancel. Hold. Reheat.* No option that would reorient reality. Her order was frozen on a grey *Pending* notice and a red *Component Empty.* Perhaps it was like when the QA interface got stuck. They probed inside the rubber casing and found a maintenance reset. The pad darkened and flashed again. *Settings.*

There – a lifeline. In the top corner, Cam checked a tiny grey box: *Floor Manager.*

One year earlier, managers had been abolished. The role was extraneous, said expert logisticians. Most managers didn't do much more than their staff. They sucked up wages for no reason. A new role system was implemented. When Tableside needed managerial authority, they were temporarily promoted. After one minute, they ceded the role to the next waiter in the queue. It worked perfectly, until it didn't.

Instead of a message window, or an irritable crew boss, Cam was presented with a timer. The pad booted into the order screen. There was Amika's booking, and a new option: *Expedited Fulfilment (VIP).*

"Do you know who I am? Do you know what I do?" Amika was seething.

"Calm down," Cam muttered. "They're only beans. It's not the end of the world."

Forty-one seconds. Forty. Thirty-nine. Thirty-eight. Cam tapped the button, and the final collapse began.

Kitchen L17 started delegating orders in a bid to catch up. Soon, L16 and L18 fell behind too. Then L15 and L19 followed. L Fulfilment sent a restock order to Central for a bean silo that had been removed months ago. Drones shot out with the last of the backstock, and found no receiving bay for their cargo. They milled from port to port, folornly pinging indifferent receivers.

Then came the VIP request. L Fulfilment passed it to Central. Central passed it to Requisitions. A cloud of drones rose from the city's industrial fringe, glittering in the killing sun. They skimmed the last rivers, toward the hydroponic towns that fed the Empire.

First one, then two, then twenty and thirty reports came back: no beans. All beds retired. From a sweltering hut on the mudflats, a rush order was pushed to the farm towns: scattered satellites where pickers lived, eking out subsistence crops on sunbaked dust. A bounty was raised – a year's wages for a sack of beans.

Drones hummed over the desert, to the furthest fringe of the Empire where a single landhold still registered the outdated crop. It was close to the border, cheek by jowl with barbarian camps beyond the fence. The flock descended and hung expectant in the heat haze. Nobody was home; only a child out raking the dust. She stopped when they clouded the sky. She had no datapad, no access to farm systems. No language in common with the machines.

They watched and waited. Beyond the fence, barbarians gathered and called to the girl in a foreign tongue. She studied the humming crows against the bright sky, bent down, and picked up a stone.

Bullets raked the dirt, and the dying earth was watered. The girl was abolished. Then, with a murmur and a roar, the fence was abolished. The drones were abolished with rocks and bottles. From the end of the line, the return began.

Word reached the farm towns first. Years they'd been kept waiting. They were ready to be repaid. They smashed requisition hubs and stormed the riverbank. The hydroponics were well defended on the outside, but internal surveillance couldn't read *sister, brother, nephew, aunt.* The pickers didn't pick for Gilgamesh, after all. Wrenches became clubs. Oil became accelerant. Drones fled in swarms back to the city.

By then, the happy people of the oasis had heard the news: silos were empty, restaurants were breaking down. Farms were burning. They overwhelmed Requisitions in panic, then stormed the municipal plaza. Vacuum tubes clogged and cracked. Underground conveyors overheated, and their custodians let them ignite.

Twenty minutes after seating, from a glass balcony among the spires of the restaurant complex, Amika and Cam watched fires bloom across the oasis city.

"Well," she said. "Don't count on a tip."

History doesn't mark who opened the reservoirs. They must have known it would not save Gilgamesh. They must have realised that the last Empire was the final price at which human survival would be bought. Green water rushed from the heart of the earth, welled up over the land, and all the rivers ran backwards.

Many months after it was all over, the kitcheners went down and settled among the ruins. They took to growing beans on the flooded bank; the First and National, to be precise.

R/L Monroe is a writer, editor and illustrator who has worked in just about every format from books and comics to live theatre and film. Born in Leith, trained as an anthropologist, and now self-employed in Glasgow, R/L has never quite figured out how to write horror stories that aren't funny or sci-fi that isn't satire. Website: mortalityplays.com.

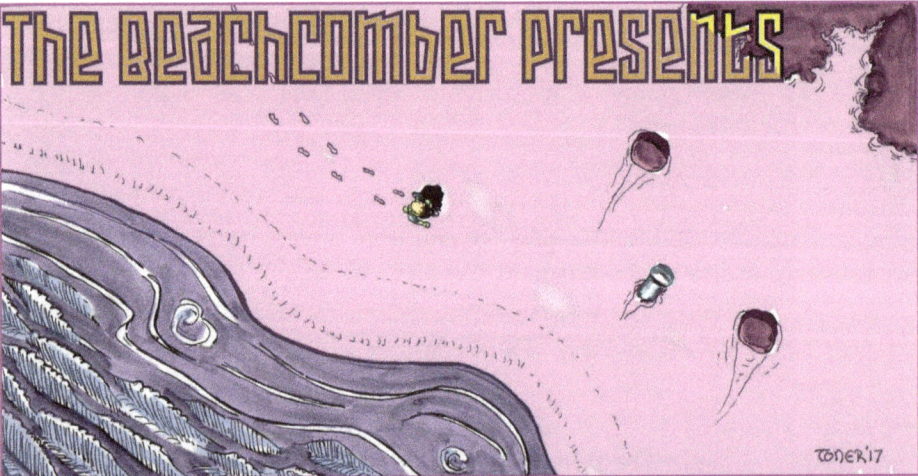

The Beachcomber Presents

WHEN IS A ROYAL MAIL PILLAR BOX *NOT* A ROYAL MAIL PILLAR BOX?

ANSWER... WHEN IT IS A *US MAIL PILLAR BOX* – A *REMINDER* OF THE RELENTLESS TINKERING OF WELL-MEANING *TIME TRAVELLERS.*

Where Have All The Time Machines Gone?

TONER'17

ONE SATURDAY MORNING...

SO IT'S LIKE *THIS...*

IF TIME TRAVEL IS *POSSIBLE* SOMEONE IN THE *FUTURE* WILL MAKE A *TIME MACHINE* AND TRAVEL INTO THE *PAST.*

THEN THERE WOULD BE TIME TRAVELLERS *EVERYWHERE!*

SOME *NATURAL PROCESS* WILL HIDE THEIR ACTIVITIES – LIKE *SEPARATING* TIME LINES.

VRRRRRRRR

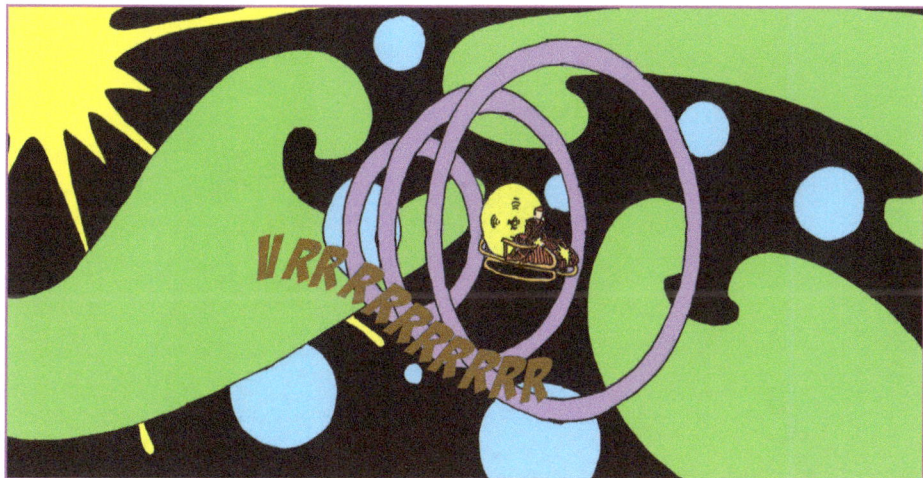

WHY INVOKE SOME *EXTRA PROCESS*? THAT JUST MAKES THE *TIME TRAVEL THEORY* ALL THE MORE *COMPLEX*.

OCCAM'S RAZOR?

GIVEN A *CHOICE* OF *HYPOTHESES*, THE *SIMPLEST* IS MOST LIKELY TO BE *CORRECT*.

TAN TATA TAN

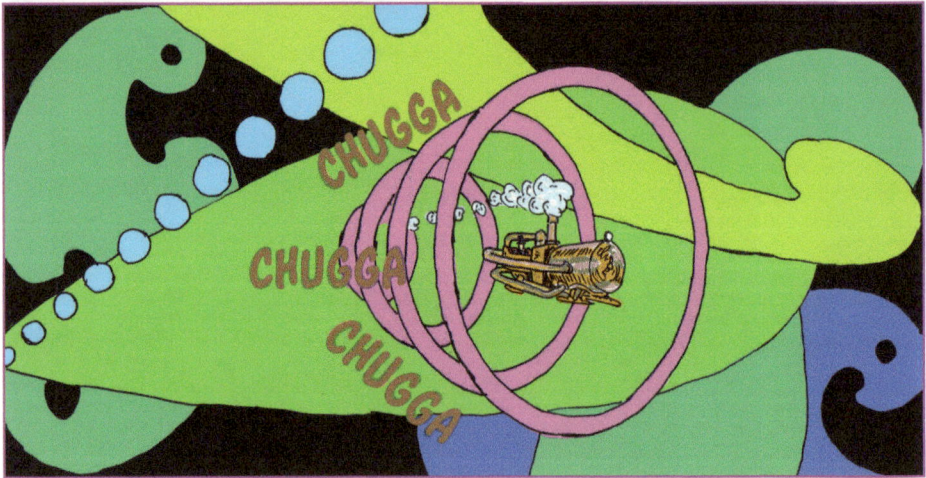

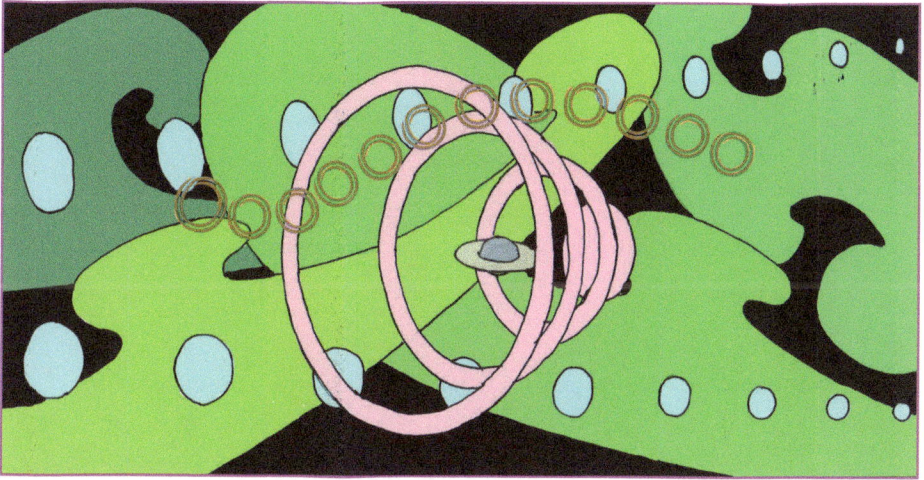

Theai

Gwyneth Findlay

'The giant impact hypothesis [proposed that] toward the end of the planetary accumulation process, the protoearth collided with a planetary body having a substantial fraction of its mass.' [1]

'The Moon is thought to be the product of such a Giant Impact. [...] I refer to this extinct impacting Moon-forming parent planet by the name 'Theia', the mother of Selene, the Greek Goddess of the Moon.' [2]

[1] Cameron, A.G.W. 'From interstellar gas to the Earth-Moon system'. Meteoritics & Planetary Science, Vol. 36, No. 1 (2001). 13.

[2] Halliday, Alex N. 'Terrestrial accretion rates and the origin of the Moon'. Earth and Planetary Science Letters, Vol. 176, No. 1 (2000). 21.

I was born the same way you were: amid violent collisions in a hot plane of swirling gas, the accretions of our dead elders coming together to form new life. The fabric of my being danced for millennia around a rapidly expanding ball of fusion and flame, forming and crashing and growing anew among billions of bits of other one-day masses, all bound wild and steady in this new sun's orbit.

Once, I was small. I was tiny. I was a speck of dust. I was shaken by passing clumps of matter, tossed about in the expanse until I met other specks of dust. They too were me, and together we became a clump, like a pebble, like a nugget, like nothing we had known before. And then our – my – clump met another clump, and it was also me, and in the shock of our meeting we became one.

I continued to assemble myself, my pieces encountering each other in the vast cloud of dust and saying, *Oh, it's you! You're me! We're us!* The invitation reached every piece of me suspended near my orbit, beckoning each fragment to come home.

Sometimes I was cold, so cold I could not explain my sensations. Other times I was brutally hot, daring fate with my uneven shuffle through the cosmos. I swung to and fro as my siblings coalesced around our Mother Sun. I passed them by, near or far: the gaseous giants that spun rapid, rambunctious; the molten balls of rock that never strayed far from the sun's hot comfort. Our nursery raged with chaos, but our family, at last, was forming. After a thousand eras as particles in the ether, we had found the pieces of ourselves. We had found each other.

We were all the same age, cosmically speaking. Mother Sun was our centre, our vitality, our *raison d'être*, but we were not born of her, as children are often born of mothers. This sun and her children sprung from the same stuff: our molecular cloud collapsed, and a family emerged.

Young and mischievous, we played together, craving camaraderie. Yet Mother Sun kept us separated in her domain, circling her at different speeds and distances. On occasion, more infrequently than the flare of a distant comet, she allowed us to align for the briefest moment, for a whisper of this existence. Then we returned to our paths, our balance across her pocket of sky.

One of my fellow rocky planets twirled near to the sun, though not so close that she became brittle or choked with gas. Her region was comfortable, even; warm and illuminated. After my initial journey from the outskirts toward Mother Sun, I danced circles along this sister's orbit, at times so intimately that I could feel the heat radiating from her fiery surface. I was so much smaller than her, and I had so little to offer in return. I simply rejoiced in the moments I could be near her, could exchange cosmic companionship amid the fury smouldering across our young sky.

We spoke of the future, of our aspirations for the time after we all settled into our rhythms among the stars. What would we do? Who did we hope to be? In my fantasy, a calm eternity stretched ahead of us, the routine of communal life spinning happily along until Mother Sun expanded and reclaimed many of our family's scattered parts into her whole. My sister, though, held wondrous visions: of love, of life, of children more numerous than all the suns of the galaxy.

Her revelation disquieted Mother Sun, and titterings about her prospects spread among our siblings. I came to learn that the vitality my sister desired was unlikely, even impossible, on her dry, fiery surface. The distant bodies whispered about a bond of hydrogen and oxygen, a molecule essential for facilitating this life she sought. Yet this building block only developed far from Mother Sun's warming glow, in the region where I came into being. I examined myself and found it: the water my sister lacked. The bitter luck of formation, of finding my parts in the gaseous sea, had bestowed it upon me while my sister was barren.

I cradled this burdensome discovery for many rotations. I could not bear to conceal this sole hope until the end of our time. In the dark, lonely patches of our sky, I devised a solution.

I said farewell to my siblings, though they did not realise it was goodbye. I waited until each one had passed, until I had sent my love to the very reaches of Mother Sun's solar expanse.

Lastly, to my most beloved sister, I said,

I love you.

I'm sorry.

Remember me.

She did not have time to react. We were moving so quickly, and I'd manoeuvred myself so close. Mother Sun, powerless but desperate, whipped plasma into my path, as if the magnetic pulse could interrupt my indomitable trajectory. My tiny body collided into my sister's side, and I became nothing but chunks of rock and clouds of dust.

Debris exploded from my sister, too, but she was not devoured. As we whirled along her orbit, her mass gained control of our distant fragments. Parts of me became parts of her, coalescing under her gravitational influence, and what remained created something entirely new: a moon, large and looming, circling her as I had once circled Mother Sun. It spun, then slowed, its face steadily focused on her, on *us* – now siblings bound as one, two beings in two bodies yet separated by none.

After millions of orbits in these new forms, the rumours proved true: life, that impossible endeavour, sprang up from our oceans. It evolved in billions of ways, sometimes slowly, sometimes all at once. Some grew to know us, to embody the love that had brought them into being. They named us – their home – Earth, and our second body they called Moon. Many of their years passed before they remembered me; the old me, as I had been before my sacrifice made us whole. They named me Theia, after the Moon's mother in one of their fading cosmologies. Now I dream of embracing each human and saying: *I am* the Moon, and you are my child, and my love begat all the life you've ever known.

Gwyneth Findlay is a writer and editor living in the North East. Her writing has appeared in The Hellebore, The Primer, and the Aberdeen-based Leopard Arts.

Find her around the internet @ findlaypum.

Theia was first published in The Primer, 2023

Gay Hunter (extract)

James Leslie Mitchell (writing as Lewis Grassic Gibbon)

She looked round the room and its sham antique oak, all solemn lines of fiddley curlicues. A great sloped mirror showed herself. Being still very young, she looked at that self with attention, but not too much. The room was deserted but for the waiter bringing the soup. Then she saw Houghton enter.

He had changed from hiking-dress—perhaps he had carried that lounge suit in the rucksack. It certainly looked a trifle crumpled. And as certainly it improved his appearance. Gay drank soup and looked at him with a faint interest—he had good shoulders and a straight back, and the cool hauteur and rangy straightness of the English Army officer of myth and rumour. As good almost as meeting an ancient Mayan in the flesh.

Funny how much better the lounge suit was than the hiking-shirt and shorts. But she'd thought that often of the feeble attempts at rationalisation in clothes that men and women made. The scantier the garments, the more feeble and ridiculous and lewd the wearers looked. The Victorians were perfectly right and logical, bless their padded bottoms. Either you clothed yourself or you went naked. To sling shorts or the various pieces of a bathing suit over this and that portion of your anatomy was to make those portions suspect and taboo....

Houghton was standing beside her. He was stiff. "I understand the waiter would like us to share a table and save him work. Lazy old devil. Do you mind?"

Gay shook her head, eating tepid fish. "I don't think so. "She turned away her eyes from another fasces badge, in the lapel of the lounge suit collar this time. "How's the headache?"

He sat down, half in profile. It was a stern, good, absurd profile. "Gone for the time being; but no doubt it'll come back. ...No, damn you, I told you I didn't want soup. A chop, man."

This was to the waiter. He shook a little, old and servile. Gay gently restrained herself from flinging the remains of the tepid fish at the correct, absurd profile. She had often to restrain herself over bodily assault in matters like that. The damned horror of any animal addressing another like that! Then she saw the twist of Houghton's face. Poor idiot.

She said: "There's a stunt in sleep-making that my father and I used to use when we went digging down in CentralAmerica. Ever hear of a man J. W Dunne?"

"Eh? . . . No."

"He's not a quack doctor or a psychoanalyst. He wrote a book called *An Experiment with Time,* and Father got hold of it. If you develop the trick you can get to sleep quite easily—unless you grow too interested in tomorrow morning."

"Oh."

But Gay was not discouraged. It was two or three years since she herself had tried those experiments at the edge of sleeping to peer into the doings of the next day or so. Father had given it up. He had said it was dangerous without elaborate precautions— funny father, the sternest and best of materialists!—salt of the earth, the materialists, though there *was* all this half-witted outcry against them these days from the sloppily superstitious Quakers who masqueraded as physicists...Well, this was how...

The old waiter sighed, peering round the edge of the door. That young 'un from America was at it with the gentleman. Bit sharp, the gentleman, but you supposed he couldn't be blamed. You were getting old, and a bit deaf, though it made you run cold to think of that, and that the boss would get to know... He looked again. Still at it, she was.

Houghton said, "Sounds rubbish. How can you look into the future—into a time that doesn't exist?"

Gay shrugged. She was a little bored herself, by now. This bleak militaristic intelligence always bored her—made flirting with ship officers and gendarmes impossible. Kind of people who never thought of the thrill of a kiss as the moment before lips touched, but just the contact and crush and a greedy suction... "The point seems to be that events don't happen. They're waiting there in the future to be overtaken."

He said "Rubbish," again grumpily; then jabbed at his chop and was suddenly loquacious.

"By God, there would be something worth while if one *could* have a glimpse of the future—project oneself into it for no more than a blink. All this modernist botching of society and art and civilisation finished, and discipline and breed and good taste come into their own again. Worth while trying half a night of sleeplessness to see that."

Gay had been about to rise and have her coffee on the verandah; but now she could not, looking at him with bent brows.

"Is that what the future is to be?"

"Of course it is. Service, loyalty. Hardness. Hierarchy. The scum in their places again." His face twitched. "England a nation again."

"And beyond that?"

"What would there be? Some dignity in history; the national cultures keeping the balance..."

Gay whistled. "Poor human race! Is that its future? Well, whatever's awaiting it, I know it isn't that."

"Some Amurrican Utopia instead, with every nation denationalised and the blah of your accent all over the globe?"

"That's just rudeness."

He coloured, stiffly. "I'm sorry."

Gay said: "Even tomorrow won't show a glimpse of anything as bad as that. Or beyond it. If we sat down tonight and tried to glimpse the future, we'd find most things we expect haven't happened..."

"All right. Let's put it to the test tonight, according to the formula of this chap Dunne that your father developed. Lie and try a glimpse into the future—and see if it's your Utopia or a sane history that the future's going to hold."

Gay said: "Of course that's just fantastic. You can see only a little of your own future—through a glass darkly."

He was holding his head again. He was really ill, Gay thought. He said, with the rudeness of pain and unease: "Afraid, like most softies, eh?"

Gay knew it was silly, but also the project was a little intriguing. She shrugged. "All right. Let's. But—if we manage to see anything at all—how are we to know when we compare results that each is speaking the truth?"

"I'm not a liar."

Gay nodded, rising. "Lucky man. Well, I'll be seeing you."

IV

The heat grew more stifling as the night wore on. Ascending to her room at eleven, Gay found the warmth swathing the place like a thick close blanket. "Like Coleridge's pants, in fact." Coleridge provided one of her gayest memories:

'As though the earth in thick fast pants
were breathing'

"Poor planet, how it must have perspired! And I feel a bit like it myself."

She took off her dress and step-ins and kicked off her shoes and sat with her hands clasping her brown knees, and looked out at the hot, stagnant night of the Wiltshire Downs. Below, she heard the old waiter closing up for the night, and the sound of heavy footsteps enter the room next her own. She thought: "The haughty Britisher with the headaches," and sat remembering their pact. The foolishest thing—especially as she didn't feel in the least in the mood for trying a neo-Dunne test to-night... She picked up the newspaper she had brought unread from the smoking-room and opened it and began to read. The night went on. At midnight she heard the clocks chime below, and woke to the lateness of the hour with a little start:

What a world! Hell 'n' blast, what a world!—as Daddy used to say in moments when it vexed him overmuch. The cruelty, the beastliness, the hopelessness of it. Not for herself—she stretched brown and clean, and looked down at herself and liked herself and thought of her lovely job among the remains of the Antique Americans and her plan for a couple of babies, not to mention a father for them, and for reading a million books and seeing a million sunrises. But she was only one, and a fortunate one... All the poor folk labouring at filthy jobs under the gathering clouds of war and an undreamed tyranny—what *had* they to live for? Even she herself—would she always escape? Unless she hid from her kind in the busy world of men, sought out some little corner and abandoned life like the folk at Rainier, like the hermits of the Thebaid. Those children of hers—would they escape the wheels and wires of life any more than the children of others? Or their children thereafter, and so on and on, till the world was one great pounding machine, pounding the life out of humanity: making it an ant-like slave-crawl on an earth turned to a dung-hill of its own futilities. She thought of Houghton next door—he was more than Houghton, he was the brutalised and bedevilled spirit of all men, she thought. And for them and their horrific future they expected women to conceive and have fruitful bodies and bear children...

Suddenly the night outside seemed to crack. Sheet lightning flowed low and saffron down over Pewsey, lighting up the Downs, and flowing soft in the foliage of the trees. Gay went to the window and watched. The earth looked a moment like a sea of fire, as though that Next War's bombardments were opening their barrage. It was hotter than ever.

She got into her sleeping-suit, put out the light, and lay down with only a sheet covering her. So doing, the view of the night vanished, for the windows were high in the wall. She stretched her toes and put her right arm under her head in the fashion that always so helped her to sleep, and closed her eyes.

Half an hour later she had tried most positions conceivable and inconceivable. But the newspapers were haunting her from sleep. She got up and drank a glass of water—tepid water that seemed to have dust in it. Low down over Upavon the thunder was growling dyspeptically. She lay down again, throwing off the sheet this time, and lay open-eyed, staring into the darkness, young, and absurdly troubled, she told herself, a little whipper-snapper absurdly and impudently troubled over a planet that wasn't her concern... Except that she hated the thought of those babies of hers, in the times to be, coughing and coughing up their lungs as the war-gas got into them...

It was only then that she remembered again her pact with the Fascist, Houghton.

V

Dreams, and a floating edge of mist. (But you must not dream. You must stay just on the edge of sleep, concentrating. So that you might awake and jot down your impressions of the pictures.) She tried to rouse herself, but a leaden weight seemed pressing now on her eyelids. Yet again she told herself not to dream.

Outside the lightning flashed, forked lightning as she knew through her closed eyelids. But now the dream-pictures were mist-edged no longer, they were jagged like the lightning. She knew herself caught in a sudden flow of images she had never tapped before—slipping and sliding amidst them like a diver going over Niagara. Something suddenly snapped and the pictures ceased...

Bombardment. The sky burst and showered the earth with glowing meteors. Great-engined monsters roared athwart the earth. Tribes fled and hid in dim confusion and climbed out again to the burning day. Great temples rose to insane creeds, and gangs of red dwarfs laboured at titanic furnaces. Peace flowed and flowered with winking seasons, season on season. Then again the sky broke and flared with terror. Now faster and faster went her fall over and into an unthinkable abyss, in a wink and flow of green and gold and jet. Ceaseless and ceaseless.

Then something smote athwart the rapids, and the pit opened and devoured her.

2. The Incredible Morning

I

SHE OPENED her eyes and saw that it was not yet dawn. There was a pale light all abroad the great stretches of the Wiltshire Downs, forerunner of the sunlight, but only a ghost of its quality. A little rain was seeping away into the east. She heard the patter of its going, light-footed, through the darkness into the spaces where the east was wanly tinted. She sat up.

Close at hand a curlew called.

She was aware that she was still dreaming, for the window of the room in the 'Peacock' was set high in the wall, so that, lying in bed, as she lay now, she could see nothing of Pewsey or the Downs beyond. This was a fragment of night-time dream. Drowsy, she lay back again, cuddling her face in her arm, and reaching out her left hand to draw up the sheets about her. Her fingers strayed uncertainly, finding no sheet. With a sleepy irritation she sought further, and then sat up again. There was no sheet. But something else had led her to sit erect. Her hand had touched her own skin.

She was naked.

She put out her hand in the dimness and touched the bed. It was not a bed. She was lying on a bank of earth—a grassy bank. It was wet with dew. Her back and legs were wet and chilled with the dew. She sat erect, very rigid, her hands behind her.

The curlew called again, very close at hand. Wings flapped in the dimness, darkness-shielded, and there came a splatter of something in a hidden pool. Gay put up her hand to her mouth and bit it.

She gave a cry at the realness of the pain. What was it? Where...?

Hell 'n' blast, she knew! Sleep-walking! Not that she had ever sleep-walked before, that she knew. But that was what it must be. She had got out of her room and out of the 'Peacock,' and wandered out to the country beyond Pewsey. What a mess!

She rubbed her chilled self and put up a hand to push back the hair from her forehead. Soon be quite light—probably not yet four o'clock. She must get back. With a little luck she might get back unseen. The labourers' wives would just be stirring to light

123

their morning fires.

She stood erect; and instantly sat down, gasping. There was something strange in the morning air that caught at her lungs, icily as though she had swallowed a mouthful of snow. Now she became aware of another fact—the rate at which her heart was beating. It was pounding inside her chest, insanely, and the blood throbbing in her forehead with the rapid beat of a dynamo. Sleep-walking and nightmare—Oh, what a fool!

She sat with her head in her hands, giddy, till the world about her began to quiet into unquivering outlines. Her heart was easing to normal pulsations. Through her fingers she saw the dawn coming on Pewsey.

And there was no Pewsey.

II

She sat in a great dip of the Downs, grassy and treeless, houseless, without moving speck of life, that she could see, north, south, east or west. In the coming of the sun great hummocks at a distance shed themselves of shadows, they seemed like great tumuli as the light came upon them. A wind was coming with the light, and blew cold with dew. But it changed and grew warmer, blowing upon her naked body, blowing her hair about her face. Below the little incline on which she sat a stream that wandered through the great hollow in the Downs lost itself in a reed-fringed stretch of water: she saw that it was a marsh-fringed loch, stretching its reeds away to the foot of the tumuli.

She began to weep, terrified and lost, watching that bright becoming of the day. Hell 'n' blast, she was mad—mad, or in a nightmare still. Where was her room and her clothes and that report on Toltec pottery?

She closed her eyes, sticking them fast, gripping her head in her hands. Then she dropped them and opened her eyes. She gave a low cry.

A great beast had come snuffling up the hill from the reeds and stood not a yard away from her, gigantic in the half-light, with pricked ears and a drooling tongue. Its musk smell smote her like a blow. It had the bigness of a bear, though the shape of a wolf. It gave a low wurr and dropped one ear.

Gay screamed, piercingly.

At that the beast backed away, growled blood-curdlingly, then turned, clumsily, and trotted away. Gay watched it with a breathless disbelief as it entered the reeds. A grunt and yap emerged. The reeds ceased to wave and move. Gay's frozen silence went.

"Lost, lost—oh, I'm lost!" She screamed the words, knowing that someone would come and shake her awake and help her— the chambermaid, perhaps. She stared about her wide-eyed, waiting that coming. The day brightened and grew.

No smoke. No sign of a house or of human habitation. She raised her eyes to the east and saw against it a moving dot. It grew and enlarged, coming earthwards and nearer. She held her breath.

It was a great bird the size of a condor, and something of the same shape, with a crooked beak and immense pinions that beat the air with the noise of a river paddle-boat. It might have been twelve feet from wing-tip to wing-tip. It planed down close to the earth, to the spot where Gay stood and glared, uttered a raucous and contemptuous "Arrh," and wheeled up into the sky again.

A condor *in England!*

Gay began to talk to herself. At the first word the silence of the deserted countryside seemed to intensify, listening. Breathtaking and terrible.

"I don't care! This isn't real, but I won't go mad! I won't, I..." She realised she was dreadfully thirsty, her lips grimed as with ancient dust. She glanced down at her body and saw it the same, covered evenly as with a thin sprinkling of soot. With a desperate courage she looked towards the loch. The beast...?

She picked up a stone in each hand and ran down into the water. It caught her and almost choked her, deep. She dropped the stones and splashed and swam, gasping. Something in the water caught at a foot, slimily, but she kicked it away. When she swam back to the shore again and climbed, gasping, from the icy embrace of the water, and wrung that water from her hair and wiped it from breasts and body and legs, she felt as though she had sloughed more than the covering of brown soot-dust. Wiping the water from her eyelashes, she raised her head again, knowing that surely the icy dip would have restored her sanity as it had cleansed her body. Around her were the unfamiliar, treeless, uninhabited hills. Then she saw something white rising up from the foot of the incline where she herself had awakened. It elongated and stretched, cruciform-wise. It was suddenly rigid. It was a man, naked as herself, and staring at her with dazed and astounded eyes.

It was Major Ledyard Houghton.

III

Her first impulse was to turn and run. But that was one too ridiculous to follow. Absurdly, she remembered a story from some Victorian romance of the heroine, nude, discovered by a man, and the modest female covering her face with her hands to hide her *identity*...She giggled and sank down on the grass.

"Thank goodness there's someone else in this mess. But however have we got into it?"

"Damned if I know. I woke and saw you swimming down there... if I am awake."

"Don't worry about that. I've thought it all out for myself, and you can take the results on trust. But I do wish you'd sit down."

"Why?"

Gay clasped her knees with her hands. "So that we can talk. And you're rather—undraped." He had an exceedingly white skin. It turned a rich crimson, face, neck... Gay turned away her eyes, politely, from survey of its further possibilities. He slumped down in the grass.

"Oh, damn it!"

He leapt up again. He had sat on a gorse-bush. Gay put up her hands to her eyes and giggled helplessly.

Giggling, she heard him say, hardly, "If you've got hysterics, you can get out of them. I'm off to see what's happened."

He was. He had jumped to his feet again. He had broad shoulders and shapely hips, except for one with a great scar, like that of a branding-iron, across it. Gay stared at the scar, herself standing up. "Where can you go? ... And where did that happen to you?" He stared over his shoulder, angry and ludicrous. "Eh?

What? What happen?" He coloured again, richly. "War-time wound."

"I see. And where are you going?"

"To find..." he stared around, "some house."

"Does it look as though there are any?"

It did not. The fact seemed to sink into their unevenly beating hearts. It was a land wild and forgotten. No human feet had trodden it, or voices called here, or the busy world of men reached out a hand here for long ages. The sunlight ran its colours up and down the near hills, gay with gorse. Far off a peewit wailed its immemorial plaint. There was no mark of cultivation or sign of human kind. Gay said, very quietly:

"Something has happened to us. I don't know what. But we're here, lost, as though we'd been newly born. If we're going to search out anything, perhaps we'd best do it together." She shaded her eyes with her hand, looking towards the tumuli. Without much hope: "There might be something to help us in those mounds."

They set out, almost side by side, across the spring of the grass. In Gay's mind was a bubbling tumult of thought and speculation, backgrounded by a horrible fear which she closed away. That wouldn't help, she'd to keep sane; and keep up with the headache man; and be thankful she'd a decent figure under these shy-making circumstances.

She glanced down at it, nicely browned, and felt absurdly cheered. Houghton swung beside her in silence, his neat, thinned Greek profile rigidly towards her, his eyes fixed ahead. She suddenly realised that he was elaborately and painstakingly *not* looking at her. Also, that he was wishing, with an angry embarrassment, that she would not look at him.

They came in silence to the foot of the great mounds. There were three of them, matted in long, coarse grass. Gay went through the space between the nearer two and saw beyond merely such rolling hill-country, rolling deserted to the horizon's edge, as lay to the west. She heard Houghton breathing, coming round the corner.

"They're just hills."

Gay shook her head. "Mounds, I think. I've dug ancient ones in Mexico, and they've much these shapes, ruined buildings with a thousand years or so of the blowing of sand and earth on the top of them..." She stopped, appalled. "Oh, God!"

He barked, "Eh?"—it must have been his tribal war-cry staring about him. But Gay was merely looking blankly at the mounds. She said:

"I don't know much of the Pewsey country, but there were no mounds near the village last night. None marked on any archaeological map. If these have taken years to accumulate, then..."

For the first time their eyes met, and she saw herself globed in the light grey eyes of Houghton—shallow, puzzled eyes, faintly red-rimmed. She saw her face, strained and white, in that reflection, above her brown throat... Houghton looked away.

"Then this can't be the Pewsey district."

"But it is. That hill over there—I saw it as I went to sleep last night—if it was last night." She felt suddenly breathless and sat down. "Listen, what did you do when *you* went to bed last night?"

"What? Tried the formula of this Dunne rubbish you talked about."

"Did you have any success?" Gay's voice sounded far away to herself. "Stuff like nightmare after a bit. Half-dozing, I suppose. The lightning cracked into the stuff and made my headache twice as bad. Then I slipped into the stuff again—damned rubbish. Woke up and saw you."

"This rubbishy dream stuff—did you have a sensation of going at a tremendous rate—slipping over the brink of a precipice?"

He scowled in thought. "No. Something—like going up a spiral staircase, and lights winking in and out from the windows. Anyhow, what does it matter? What's it to do with this—blasted insanity?"

"I'm not sure—yet.' Gay Hunter still felt breathless. That, and queer, as though she was about to be sick. "But I've a guess—oh, hell 'n' blast, it can't be, it can't be!"

"All this is rot to me. Look here, if we're going together, we might as well start. I'm going on—to get clothes somewhere, and back to London, whatever has happened here in Wiltshire."

Gay stood up, slowly, a queer look on her face. "All right? East?"

"That's the direction of London, isn't it?"

"Yes, that's the direction of London. Or was."

"Eh?"

She gripped his naked arm. "What's *that?*"

That was a movement in the long grass at a distance of ten yards or so from the mounds—a movement that ended in a tall, blonde woman, unclad as themselves, with a scared, astounded face, rising into full view and staring at them with horrified eyes. Gay blinked her own eyes at the sight. Had the whole damn landscape been showered with undraped females in the night? O Lord, she was going mad...

"*Ledyard!*"

Houghton stood halted, staring, a dismayed, agonised, smoking-room-story blush in effigy.

"Jane!"

Gay slumped down in the grass, too wearied with surprises even to giggle. "Do introduce us."

"Eh? What? Oh *Lord*, Jane! ...This is Lady Jane Easterling, Miss Hunter."

The author of *Gay Hunter* was James Leslie Mitchell (1901-1935). If you don't recognise this name, you're more likely to be familiar with his nom-de-plume, Lewis Grassic Gibbon.

Find out more by reading James Leslie Mitchell by M J Burns. This is published on SF Caledonia at

www.sfcaledonia.scot/james-leslie-mitchell-aka-lewis-grassic-gibbon-by-m-j-burns/

Take the QR code for a shortcut.

How Yer Glaikit Gran Beat Back The Beat

Callum Dougan

See in Graveside? Two things killed folk. Thae things were the drink and the Beat: I didnae drink. As for the Beat? My stolen steel toes tip-tappin – they aw felt it, the entire bar. Vibrations flowin through the floor, countin four-four? That's how it starts. Once it spreads ye're doomed tae repeat, like Jimmy Hauns the week afore. He tapped oot efter a day's worth, died with forty fingers wedged in dents they'd drummed in the toon lamppost. People said *Well. That's what ye get. Robbin the Graves and ye dare greet? Easy come, easy go.*

Mark stepped back, cleanin a glass. He frowned at the bloody cheek of me. 'Away wi ye.' In aw fairness? The

Bonehoose didnae need mair Beat, judgin by the crumblin ceilin. Mark was auld and he kent the Beat: how folk caught it and how that'd go and why we went doon there still. So he jist shrugged. 'Take the bottle. But ye're scarin the patrons see.' Easy come, easy go.

'So ye're sayin,' I summarised, ' "oot afore the Beat drops" of course?' I had naewhere – other than there – tae sit waitin for the facin. But his fingers tapped staccato. And he was giein me the Look. The one that said *I cannae afford tae fix the windaes again*. I jist stood there, countin oot time. My heartbeat whispered in Auld Morse: *easy come, easy go*.

Fightin was oot. Everyone tried, and everyone endit up beat. So I figured: jist embrace it. What was the worst that could happen? They wantit me tae go die quiet? Like fu-darn would I die quiet. I'd gie them the deepest damntit drop and one hell of a show. The bottle clinked, full and too low. Poured hauf oot and made my retreat: *easy come, easy go*.

El said 'that's close enough.' I was ten feet away. She was at her windae with her big crossbow. I'd only needed scrap – naebody was lackin, not here in Graveside or anywhere bloody else. But by now the Beat was straight-up beyond hidin. My arms twitched *one-and-two-and-three-and-four-and*. They were gettin faster and faster and wait where was I oh aye El was tellin me tae go die- She looked me in the eye. 'Don't tap out like a fool. Beat only ends one way and it's one you well know: *easy come, easy go.*'

What should I have done ai? Stuck tae bloody hoppin? The deid's parts were poison but we went even so. There's a clue there weanling, a thread one day ye'll pull: how come the poison and how come we'd no forgo? How come the whole Graveside and how come aw the Graves? How come we got the Beat and how come in that place? How come everyone would jist look at ye with a stopped watch face and how come naebody dared riot? Folks wantit me quiet. But I'd gie them a show: I'd show them aw the soul in my new steel big toe: *life's easy come, life's easy go.*

Youse ever tried buildin a stage? When you're deep intae heavy Beat? And the whole toon's wantin somebody else tae take ye aff the street? I wisnae even infectious – unless some eejit stole my parts. Beat was in them aw now frae my tappin feet tae my revvin heart. In hands hammerin with syncopation and thae deep auld deid blues. In my gyroscope spinnin like a young boxer thirteen pints doon. In the hammerstrike and heartbeat and the clock of the Awmighty aw syncin up intae a chorusin wall of slick-thick tune. I couldnae let it drop too soon. There's a right time tae let it go. But the Beat didnae agree and in my soul I heard it echo: *life's easy come, life's easy go-*

But it was comin oan fiercely. So I was runnin oot of time. And I was daein that thing I dae where I cannae help but rhyme. Everything had tae be jist right. I ran a finger doon the line. Every bottle chimin tae an absolute purestrain perfection, every part of me rippin on past aw the factory settins – if they even had them afore the war and the Graves and the Beat – chimin glass and bangin steel for the evergrowin crowd of folk (brave enough tae stay and watch me and cowards enough tae stay back, like I was chock-fullae nitro). The Beat pushin me still louder, my vocaliser tearin up eighty decibels past zero: '*life's easy come, life's easy go—'*

And then I gave myself over. Jist let the Beat in and hit it. Hit it hard as I could afore it tapped me oot for ever, the steel boards whup-whup-whup-wobblin, the drop comin ever closer: I hit it and hit it and hit it but the drop jist didnae come – *impossible* they were thinkin, *nae chance she keeps this up for long* – but like hell was I done yet because I hadnae finished this song (aw I had tae dae was *go on*)-

So that's how I beat back the Beat frae the Graves deep doon deid Glasgow, and by now wean ye've heard me tell it in every key and tempo: *life's easy come, life's easy go—*

Callum Dougan was born during Voyager 2's closest approach to Neptune, so if you didn't like this story you know who to blame. Previously published in Shoreline of Infinity and Aether & Ichor, he lives in West Lothian with his two monitors and Mario Tennis for the N64.

How Yer Glaikit Gran Beat Back The Beat was first published in Shoreline of Infinity 28, 2022

Art manipulation: Olen

A Flight of Birds

E.M. Faulds

I'm hungry. How long are you supposed to leave it between feedings anyway? The question floats above my head every now and then; a scribbly little black cartoon cloud with lightning bolts and knives stabbing out of it. For a cloud, it's heavy. It stands up against the fug of the coffee house as the espresso machine gently farts and hisses disapprovingly at my side. I'm hungry. But, more importantly, Jimmy's late.

I lean low over the counter, check the light levels through the steamed-up glass frontage behind Mr Chowdhury. The space around the black and orange curlicue font decals is still dark. No need to panic, yet. He sips from the tiny cup of cortado that he takes after his shift at the all-night newsagent and rustles a paper with the headline 'Police Baffled'. We never talk while he's sitting. It suits us both that way — he likes to wind down and I don't like talking too much. It shows my teeth. Don't worry, I'd never bite him. Then there'd be no-one in here for large swathes of time and that would be worse than the hunger. And besides, he's silent, but it's the good kind, the amiable kind. I don't think he's ever hurt anyone in his life. But the world outside the coffee shop? That's a different story.

Byres Road, West End, Glasgow. This time of night it's nose-to-tail parked cars. Cycle back a couple of hours and it's jumping, filled with entrepreneurs talking about engagement dynamics on their way to a craft beer popup, managing directors pushing past students in the plethora of vegan cafes, bus after bus, drunkards struggling back to the subway after the work's night out, or the people so lost in their lives they can only express themselves through a ragged, existential yawp. And I get to deal with them all on a nightly basis. But from now until end of shift, it's Monday-night quiet. Morning will come and the machine winds up again until all you can hear is the buzz of people and the rumble-shake of the train tunnel under your feet. Not that I get to see that.

04:30. A time etched onto the leathery surface of my heart. It's the earliest the sun ever rises in Glasgow. If I'm not home that time around the solstice, I've got drama coming. By July, August, there's some play. Two extra minutes of darkness every morning. A wee buffer if it's raining, which it usually is. By winter, I'm golden. Some days it's as if the sun just doesn't bother. But it's May, the sunniest weather, and I've got to be careful.

The angry growls of hunger in my stomach are making me obsess-spiral. As far as I know, there's no reason to worry.

Don't get me wrong, I don't want to kill anybody, but my urge to bite is rubbing at me like sandpaper. It's a pain that never goes away. Neither do the cold fingers, even now in summer. I'm reliably informed it gets roasting in here when the espresso machines are going full bore in the middle of a July day, but I'll not get to find that out. I told Scott I was studying palaeontology at Uni so I could never do daytimes, always had to be out the door by 04:00 at the latest. He never wondered when exactly I'd sleep, and I only have to endure the occasional quiz about what the best dinosaur is. ("Well, you see Scott, the more you learn about them, the more you realise they're all special in their own way.") And the nickname DG. For "Dino-girl".

Mr Chowdhury brings back his wee cup and saucer with a smile. His neat moustache has a little smoosh of froth on it, but I don't want to embarrass him. "Goodnight, darling, or should I say good morning?" He always makes the same joke and always calls me darling because he thinks it's a nice thing to say to a woman. I tell him I'll see him tomorrow and he's off home.

I'm alone again for a while, only the wall-clock and the espresso machine's conversation with itself marking time. I wonder what's waiting for Mr Chowdhury at home. A quiet, sleeping household of warm beds? A bare mattress in a flat above the shop? The ghost of cooking clinging to the soft furnishings or a wreckage of take away containers? You never know what goes on in someone else's home. And I can never get close enough to ask.

The vanishing people. That's what they should call us. Hotel staff, refrigerated lorry drivers, bartenders, office cleaners, alkies, call centre workers, cops, and robbers. People who vanish from the daytime world's consciousness. We may as well not exist as far as they're concerned. But we exist for each other. There's recognition in their eyes, relief when they see there's space and peace here for them. And they have absolutely no idea what they mean to me.

A baobhan sith's never born. They're made. My maker was some old prick in Queen's Park who lurched out of the bushes. I thought he was just a homeless person off his face on Buckie, so put my black belt in Taekwondo to good use and sent him back into the bushes. But before he disappeared, I got a scratch off one of his teeth on my little finger. Not a bite. Not a sensual clinch of neck nibbling that looks pure like sex. No, a bit of a tear. I've had worse cuts making a sandwich. And that was it.

Adrenaline and shock made me go to the out-of-hours clinic at the Victoria, but they just gave me a bandage and stuck my arm with a needle the size of a drinking straw, "Just to be sure." I didn't bother going to the police. I told the medical staff it had been an accident. What was I going to say? That I'd kicked a homeless guy in the baws?

I went home. It was there, tucked up in my own bed, that the wrongness came down on me.

A long time later, I cottoned on to the fact it's not just passed on to anybody. That there has to be something else. Something inside you that says, *enough*.

There are customers who come in during the wee hours that don't fit the late-night crowd so neatly. Like her. She works both days and nights, gets to walk both sides of Glasgow's darkness and light. I don't know her, but she comes in wearing purple scrubs and orders one of those coffee cups as big as your heid. She sits at a small table by the power sockets, typing on her laptop for up to three hours. Sometimes she's there as I come on shift, sometimes as I'm about to go off. I know the name on her debit card is Miss C. Thompson. Whatever the 'C' stands for, she doesn't look like she wants to be a Cathy or a Claire, fingers thumping at the keyboard so fast it's like a hailstorm on a garden shed. Maybe a Charlotte or a Cordelia, maybe a Celeste. It's one of those initials that can swing right through the spectrum from hard to soft. But I just think of her as C.

In the intricate daydreams I have during a shift, C knows all about my condition. She's constantly pestering me to come forward and share my condition with science and get on the telly and I have to regretfully refuse, saying, "I work best in darkness." In reality, I know exactly the face she would put on. Right before she told me not to make such a stupid joke.

It's 04:45. Jimmy still hasn't come in to take the early shift. He hasn't replied to my texts and I'm getting antsy. The details of the street outside are far too crisp; the sliver of sky above the shops opposite has gone from navy to steel blue. C's still here, and

the apprentices have drifted in for their triple-shot Americanos —
showing off, bless 'em. I want to kick them all out and shut up
shop, but I don't think I'd have a job tomorrow if I did. And he
said he'd be here.

"C'mon, Jimmy," I mutter and jiggle from one foot to the other.
I'm so twitchy I hardly notice that C is staring at me. She has
earbuds but they must have been down low. Or she's using the
trick where she just puts them in her ears to keep people away.

She takes one of the headphones out.

"Sorry," I say, finally clocking her. "Talking to myself."

She smiles and nods awkwardly. "Sorry, I thought you were
speaking to me."

I mean, yes, that's obvious. "Sorry, no. No." This could go on
all night. I want it to stop but it's like a car crash. I watch the
words fall out of my mouth. "Just wondering where my colleague
has got to." Why do I do that? Just say no and leave it at that.

"Is your shift over?" she asks.

C, please stop.

"Yup." Me, please stop, you're no good at this. You were never
good at this. Always on the periphery of conversations, back
when you had a group of pals to hang out with. Walking between
pubs on a night out, you'd always manage to fall between the twos
and threes who were chatting arm in arm. And even those days
are just a Vaseline-smeared lens of memory, now.

"Are you going to miss your bus or anything?" She's still poised
with that earbud halfway out, tentative. Like a deer on the edge
of a forest. I guess she can see the stress lines I get on my forehead.
Or how I'm nearly dancing on the balls of my feet. "I could give
you a lift maybe?"

"It's okay, I can walk, it's not too far."

"Are you sure?" C, I'm begging you. Please stop, you're killing
me with awkwardness, and I'm basically immortal.

"No, it's fine," I smile, a closed-lips tight little smile. "I could
use the exercise. Thanks, though."

The badness. The wrongness. It came over me while I lay in bed trying to shake off the jitters after the prick in the park attacked me. I hate confrontation, spent most of my life trying to avoid it. I'm not a coward, mind. And I have a black belt in TKD. That's not easy to do. But confrontation rattles me, it takes me ages after to stop chewing it over and over. Like, how dare he? Should I have gone to the polis? I was staring at the strips of light and shadow on my ceiling, playing it over in my head, when it came down.

How to explain it? Have you ever seen that video of the deep-sea footage of a giant squid? It looms out of the black, bobs and dances for a while, caresses the camera equipment with its tentacles and drifts off. Then it comes back like a reverse explosion, all its arms pointed together like a knife and at the last second, they lunge and wrap and that's the end of the recording.

That. It's like that.

I have to ring Scott and he comes in. Jimmy's getting fired, I can tell that much by his face. "Thanks, DG," he tells me and says he'll put the extra time on my wages. I barely take the time to nod as I hang up my apron and scramble a hoody on. I've got about fifteen minutes to get half an hour across town.

I'd duck into the subway, but it won't be open for another hour. I like it down there when it's quiet. It's the safest place I could be in the daytime but it's more than that. The sound of the train is loud but that just means hardly anyone bothers talking and you can retreat into your own little world while the carriage rocks you back and forth. The stations smell like wet stone and metal, and I can't tell you why I like that, but I do.

Today, though, I have to run. I dig sunglasses out of my pocket. I'm already wearing trainers, but I've been on my feet for six hours and my backpack is full of junk that juggles about and digs into my kidneys. I consider a bus, but the routes are wrong, they'll take too long. I head down towards the river. I can follow it back to Finnieston, scarper across the bridge at the SECC.

If I could live in the West End, I would. But it's as possible for me as flying, which, no. I can't.

I try to keep to the shadows at the foot of the row of shops but soon the disadvantage of living south of the river hits me, quite literally, in the face. I pull my hood forward as far as it'll go, but it's not quite enough.

I remember blundering into the sunlight when I was just new. I mean, it really hadn't sunk in. I wasn't thinking, walked smack bang into broad daylight. Not for long, mind, but long enough.

There's no baobhan sith support group to tell you what to do. I didn't even know what I was. I thought it was classic vampirism all the way, the Bela Lugosi stuff. To be fair, a lot of it basically works the same. But Scotland's always had a history of blood-drinkers. True, the folklore that accreted around it is mostly wrapped up in transparently sexist bullshit.

Some men go get pished in a little isolated hut, a shieling. They start dancing, just for fun. They make the mistake of wishing for some female company and all of a sudden there's a knock on the door. A sexy lady appears. One of the men notices she has the feet and legs of a deer, so instead of warning his pals that something is up, he legs it. So, of course, Mr Lucky is the only survivor, as the rest are massacred, their throats laid open. He says it was a baobhan sith that did it and he was spared her attack because he was the only virtuous one among the group.

People believed what they wanted to back then, didn't they?

Baobhan sith means: the human plus package — not quite super-strength, but tough, not a lot going on in the heartbeat department, a shocking sunlight allergy, an outsize desire to drink blood. Tick in each of those columns. No deer feet. And no get out of jail free card for lying wee shites like the guy in the story.

Quite the opposite.

I slam through the door of the close and take the stairs two or three at a time. When I'm safe in the flat, I strip off and rush to the bathroom to sit in the tub, spraying my face with the shower hose attachment on cold.

I get out after about half an hour, inspect the damage in the bathroom cabinet mirror. (Yes, I have a reflection. If photons could pass through me, UV light wouldn't be so bloody problematic, would it?) I look like what I am — a burns victim. It's mostly confined to my cheeks and chin, some of my wrists where they weren't deep enough in my pockets. Even with the hoody and my head down, the light bounced off the pavement. Without the sunnies, I guess my eyelids would have welded shut. I touch the tender area with my fingertips and some of the top layer sloughs off with a cut-glass pain. I can't even scream because it'd stretch my lips, so I end up clenching my jaw and mewling like a kitten.

I think about calling Scott to see if I can take tonight off, but I doubt he'll let me if Jimmy got bounced from the rota. I creak the cabinet open, tired, and get the tube of aloe vera.

It takes a couple of hours of lying still, coating myself in green gel and holding a bag of frozen peas to my face while at the same time trying not to touch it at all. I don't heal per se. But the pain stops being so insistent after a while. The skin will stop peeling soon, just look like a huge rashy sunburn, which will fade back to the regular anaemic pallor eventually. But for now, I have to wait, lying here, listening to the world wake up and get on with it on the other side of my blackout curtains while I weather the pain. I want to go to sleep but every time I do, some wanker bangs the close door or beeps a horn. Every sound is too sharp, layering on top of the burns. Eventually, I grit my teeth and get out my phone for something to do. Open up Fotousi and scroll through the posts of accounts I follow. Nothing great. A few interesting ones from @mejer_playa, but it feels crap having nothing to post of my own. I try to put something up every day. Gives me that little buzz when someone likes a pic, Pavlov's dog that I am. And it feels like connection, even if it's not really real.

My account is all shots, (unsurprisingly), of the nightlife in Glasgow. I had to save up to buy my handset outright since my credit rating is so crap. But it takes the best low-light pictures. I scroll back through my own timeline, tasting each moment. It might be egotistical, but I like what I did, or I wouldn't do it. Pictures of people spilling out of bars under smeared neon and bokeh string lights; the Mitchell Library like a parliament house, a Tiffany lamp knockoff in a wee oval window in a pebbledash council house wall. I even once caught a bunch of lads making a human pyramid to put the traditional hat on the head of the statue of Wellington. I hadn't really thought how it was done before; the orange and silver traffic cone just appeared, like a snowdrop in the spring.

I should get over to the Necropolis. I promised myself a photoshoot there on a dead night. A quiet night. Just me. And the goths finger-banging up against a mausoleum, but I could work around them. Good view from the top of the hill.

I found him again. The one who bit me.

I put two and two together after the wrongness had cleared. At the time, I'd thought it was the flu. You know the type where you can barely get out of bed to pee, barely hold down fluids? Turns out it wasn't that. When I finally let myself comprehend what was going on, that I was dead but still, you know, *continuing*, I thought I might find him. When I regained my strength. To my surprise, I had a lot more strength than before. It didn't make up for being relegated to the dark, segregated from the rest of humanity, but it was useful.

I spent a lot of nights hanging out in the bushes at Queen's Park, tempted to leap out and drag some people back into the shadows myself.

But I didn't. Knowing that the urge could be resisted just made me angrier. He came along the path, looking at joggers going by, and I knew. Knew it was him. Funny thing was, he didn't even see what he'd done. He wasn't a baobhan sith, just a carrier. Just a sad fuck who preyed on people for his own thrills. Admitted to attacking girls, kids sometimes. He let that slip when I had him up against a wall two feet off the ground.

I'm not too proud of what came after.

The shop door goes and there's the *swipp* of corduroyed thighs and the clack of summer shoes as someone crosses the floor. I know before turning my head that it's C, early tonight. She's wearing a light peasanty blouse with paisley print in green, brown cords and flat sandals. Her nose, cheeks, and neckline are almost as red as my face beneath my full-coverage foundation. I guess she had a day off, maybe sat out in Kelvingrove on the grass bit where everyone ignores the outdoor drinking ban and brings a disposable barbecue. But now she's here, and there's her laptop bag. "The usual," she says, dimpling.

Number seven brew, venti latte. "I'll bring it over," I tell her as she blips her debit card.

"Cheers," she says and goes to set up her laptop. I've never managed to see what she's writing. She sits with her back to the wall. I hope it's not sparkly vampire fic.

Although, that would be something to talk about.

I used to have family. My dad hit my mum, but she wouldn't leave him, though I begged her. So, I left instead, went to Glasgow, flat shared and took shitty jobs until I could save up for a place of my own. I found some friends and I was going to make something of my life. It makes me really tired thinking about all this stuff. But yeah, I'd found a new life. And then the guy in the park, the cut on my pinkie.

How could I explain what was going on? To anyone? "Oh, by the way, I'm kind of like a vampire but more tartan"? I fobbed them off with excuses, was sarcastic, withering, utterly horrible. Until they stopped messaging. I burned my old accounts. My Fotousi handle is just a random string of letters. I don't really know why I bother with it. I guess it gives the illusion of not being alone.

I take the bus up towards the cathedral on my way to work on the Tuesday night, so I can do my photoshoot but get to my shift in good time. I hang on to a pole with my back to the bag rack and don't look anybody in the eye. I'm not unusual-looking enough to raise a comment. No deer feet or anything. Only, I'm female for all eternity.

143

I can see one of the passengers nudging his pal and pointing at me. He thinks he's being subtle. He hasn't got a handle on how peripheral vision works. I turn my shoulder as if I'm looking out the window, to put my arm as a barrier between them and my tits. (Well, what else am I going to do? On a bus?) Soon as I can, I ding the bell and scoot up to the cobbled precinct. The black spire of the cathedral pokes up into the dark denim blue of the summer night sky.

They have a gate and opening hours, which is sweet. As if it would stop any moderately determined Glaswegian. I hop the low fence at the side of the manse and get out my phone as I check around for other night-time visitors. A lot of kids come up here, trying to be edgy.

Movement. A fox trots out between the gravestones and off on his own business. He's too quick for me to get a shot. I turn the screen brightness right down on my phone and head for the path up the hill. Saints and draperies, baroque mausoleums and palatial tombs, statues to the rich and powerful. I wonder if any of the Tobacco Lords are buried with a stake through the heart.

There's a tiny rotunda that sits proud of the hillside not far from the Knox monument which I climb up to park myself, back to the base of a column. There are still the dregs of a sunset off the way I came, just a glow where the sun ducks under the horizon. I guess I'm lucky I don't live in the north, up Orkney way. Or Lapland.

I raise my phone and open the camera app, steady my elbows on my knees and start taking pictures: a Victorian angel's outstretched hand in silhouette. Moss growing out of a small spire. A tree elbows its way between graves, knocking them sideways in extreme slow motion while little birds dart in and out of the dark mass of leaves. Summertime and they don't really know what to do with themselves. A dawn chorus that barely ends. How quiet must they feel in the long winter nights, the ones who stay, the ones who don't get to fly south? Not on the cards for me either, birds.

I'm aware of the two people staggering up the path beneath the rotunda a long time before they get here. The giggles and loud shushing of people drunk enough to think they're being quiet.

She's holding onto his elbow but keeps going over on her ankles. I put my phone away and stay still as a gargoyle. It's easy for me. They don't notice. The guy is playing along, but I can see he's a lot less pished than she is. He's glancing sharply at the shadows. Not looking where I'm sitting above their heads.

She's middle aged and middle class. He's unremarkable. Remarkably unremarkable. He shoves her down on the grass. She's stunned at first. Laughs, thinks they fell over. Then she makes some confused 'what are you doing?' type noises.

I hop down from the rotunda and when I'm behind him, as he's fiddling with his zipper and trying to cover her mouth, I shout "Oi!"

He jerks his head around. His eyes are deader than mine. When he sees I'm a woman he says, "Fuck off, this is none of your business."

"I'm calling the polis," I say, loudly.

He ignores me. He knows by the time they come it'll be too late.

It's time for me to do the thing. I don't want to do the thing. But for him, I will.

I was always told women should never go out at night in Glasgow on their own. Never take a shortcut down the lanes, make sure to get in a registered taxi, make sure you can kick your heels off and run if you need it. Now I go to the dark corners, the unlit paths on purpose. What's shocking? The amount of crime that isn't reported.

I go towards the muffled struggle these days. I've got it down to a fine art. The one being held down only knows it's stopped, thinks the bad guy was scared off. It happens so quick they can't tell that it's me. Can't thank me. What I do isn't legal, and it isn't nice. I try not to do it if I can help it. And I don't like the idea of someone not facing a jury for what they did. But, at the same time, I have to feed and it isn't pretty. In fact, I kind of have to make it messy to cover up the marks.

I'm sure some of Police Scotland suspect there's a vampire in Glasgow. But they'd never say that out loud, in public.

I haven't met any other baobhan sith. I think I'd know them. I knew the one who turned me, figured out he was a carrier, but I've never had a reaction to anyone else. I'd love to meet one. Then they could tell me what the fuck I'm supposed to do with the rest of my life. Or unlife. Whatever. I mean, tearing the throats out of scumbags is something I'm good at, but it's not a *career*, you know?

And I wouldn't be so alone.

She's sobbing uncontrollably because she feels stupid. I'm holding her up so I can walk her down to somewhere safe. She's fighting the alcohol but it's winning. I don't normally let them see me, but I can't leave her here, vulnerable. And I don't think she'll be able to identify me. Her eyes aren't focusing right.

"It's okay," I say, over and over. I try to ask her if she wants to go to the police.

"He said we should go watch the sunrise," she replies. "I thought he was being romantic." She vomits copiously on her shoes. In my bag next to the balled-up, blood-soaked wet wipes, I have a little packet of tissues. I give her one. She dabs it vaguely near her lips.

I have to get to work, so I see her to the taxi rank down where the streets are well lit. I make a point of hearing her tell the driver where she lives while I take pictures of his plates. He won't try anything. I don't think she says thank you, but I really don't want her to. I keep thinking about who will find the body stuffed into that niche in the mausoleum and hate myself.

I jog to work, holding my belly as it sloshes. My physical health appreciates it, if not my spiritual.

"Good night, darling, or rather, good morning," Mr Chowdhury says. Tomorrow his paper will say 'Urban Foxes Attack Deceased in Grisly Find' or something. People always find a way to explain what they don't want to think about. I wave and give him a solemn nod while I upload the photos of the birds to Fotousi.

Those were the best of the night, before I had to break off. The shutter speed was slow, so they streak and zoom out of the tree like dark thoughts, the threat of daylight looming behind them, just over the horizon. No flying south.

Square it up, filters? Naw, it's good as is. I post and put the phone down under the counter, beside the glass latte mugs. It's quiet in the shop tonight except for C's keyboard storm, punctuated by moments where she leans back and scrolls on the mousepad with one hand and holds her huge coffee cup with the other. She clicks and her eyebrows plunge and then she snorts and smiles and clicks some more. Then back to the words.

Scott left a note on the whiteboard in the 'staff room', (a big cupboard where you can hide pretending to look for extra filters). On the board, the rotas get thrashed out. The column under the letter 'J' has been scribbled out with furious marker strokes. Then, 'DG – extra shifts?' He wants me to do more work. I wonder if he's going to try to add to my responsibilities. I'll tell him if I'm late again I'll shut up the shop. I'll say there's a relative I'm caring for. Something no-one would argue with. I get my phone out to look up obscure geriatric medical terms. Can't be too careful. He's the type to go check there really is such a thing as an Ankylosaurus.

A Fotousi notification appears on my screen: *Cassandra Thompson hearts your photograph.* I check the avatar on the account. It's her. It's C.

She's bringing her empties back to the counter. My first instinct is to hide the phone back under the counter. She doesn't know it's me. She can't. My face and name are nowhere to be seen on the Fotousi wall. There is no trail, I've made sure of that. But she looks up from balancing the cups. She sees my face. "What's up? You all right?"

I deflect. "Yeah, just funny. I…" It's easier to just show her so I shove the screen over before I can think carefully. She sees the app, my account, the photo, her heart.

Her mouth hangs open and I know the next word out of her mouth will be 'stalker', or 'weirdo', but it's not. "What are the chances?" She shifts her laptop bag onto her shoulder better. "You working to fund your artistic endeavours, too?" She nods at the apron, the espresso machine.

I shrug. "Naw… photography's just a hobby." I sound so useless I want to die. Except I can't. Did that already.

"Oh, you should do something with it. It's important. Art helps people. Brings them together. And you're really good." She looks vaguely towards the door. "I have to go, get some sleep. I'm on shift in three hours again." Lates then earlies? That's tough. I reach for her tray, but she pins me with her eyes. With her dimples. "But let me know if you're ever doing an exhibition. Or selling prints. I'd love to be your first customer."

"Th-thanks, that's very kind." I can't help but answer her grin before I remember myself and cover my teeth with my hand. She gives me a look that's puzzled but kind.

"Not at all," she says and pats the counter in farewell as she heads out.

The tingles last all the way to the end of shift. I walk home. Birds are zooming about, dark streaks against a denim-blue sky, and my Converse about two feet above the pavement. I might be getting ahead of myself, but maybe there's something to the idea of having friends. They can see stuff when you're oblivious. Believe in you when you think you're hopeless.

Maybe I'll try again. I'll do everything different this time.

E.M. Faulds is a science fiction and fantasy writer born in Australia who now calls Scotland her home. She is a member of the Glasgow SF Writers' Circle. Her short stories have been published in *Strange Horizons, ParSec, and Shoreline of Infinity* magazines, and her collection "Under the Moon" won a British Fantasy Award in 2023. Her novella, Bring Me Home, is due to be published in 2025 with Wizard's Tower Press, and she co-edited the anthology Gallus which was launched at Worldcon in 2024.

Find out more at https://emfaulds.com/

A Flight of Birds was first published in Shoreline of Infinity 25, 2022

We tell stories too

Not only a read, but a listen and a watch too. Here is a couple of examples you can find on our website. We're adding more as we grow.

Here's Debbie Cannon reading '#noBadVibes' by Katy Lennon
sfcaledonia.scot/urls/nbv

And Andrew J Wilson reading 'That Goddam Hat', accompanied by Kenny MacKay on guitar

sfcaledonia.scot/urls/tgh

First time published. This is episode one, in two chapters, of
Kirsti Wishart's terrific Superheroes romp - what if there was an
epidemic of mutants of superheroes in Scotland? Let's find out
together

The story continues online on SF Caledonia, with new episodes
published regularly.

The Pocketbook Guide to Scottish Superheroes

Kirsti Wishart

Chapter 1

A rude awakening? – Swarming superheroes – a blast from the past

I felt it before I heard it. A wave of pressure easing me over to the side of the room then the 'BOOM' hit, gave the place a shake, the anger spilling out of me, 'Christ, not *tonight -*'

I flinched, checked to see if they'd woken Mum up. Because there'd have been hell to pay if they had, I'd have been *raging*. Bloody superheroes or not, I'd be phoning the police, making a complaint.

It had been a nightmare getting her to sleep, the drugs taking ages and now the daft wee glass ornaments on the dressing table were levitating, floating a good inch above where they should be, dancing about, the mirror rattling like it was having a laugh. The aftershock shoogling the air set off a buzzing in my chest and I coughed. But Mum, thankfully, was oblivious, snoring away.

Once I'd got breath back enough to sigh, those ornaments floating back to where they should be, everything settling, I risked tiptoeing to the curtains to check the all clear. But my timing was rubbish, a blaze of white blinding me. I pulled the curtain back quick but it didn't make much difference, the walls bright like there was a bloody great lighthouse outside our top floor flat.

A second later it was back to darkness and I was whispering '*Bastards*' when a band of green crept round the edges of the window, raced about the room, stopped a few inches down the headboard above Mum's head. Was it the Northern Lights maybe? Because from what I could remember The Fenian had been banned from Dundee airspace. Whoever it was, they were being a right nuisance and as I thought that the green vanished, left her alone.

Rubbed my eyes, tried to ease the sleep away. Mum's alarm clock read 1:06am. A school night as well. I figured the drugs would keep her quiet until about 5am as long as those idiots didn't cause any more bother.

Shuffling towards her, eyes still blurry from the flash of light, I stubbed my toe on the bedside table, had to stifle my 'Oyah!' sitting heavily on the bed. After I'd fiddled with the baby monitor, I stroked the hair back from her forehead. Like the way she used to when I was wee and ill. It was nice to see the tension away from her face, the pain gone. She looked younger. Well again almost.

As she'd slept through the earlier racket I was hoping she'd make it to a decent hour without waking up. It worried me though when I was that tired. Sometimes it'd be fine and I'd hear her voice straight away, crackling with fear over the monitor, calling for Dad. Other times it would take a while for me to wake up. I'd only know she needed me when my dreams turned bad.

Like I was on this big weird wooden boat and Dad was somewhere below decks but there's a storm at sea and Mum's out there in the waves, trying to swim but drowning slowly and I have to decide who I'm saving and when my hand grips the rail, I wake up.

I yawned wide enough for my jaw to crack. At least there hadn't been the usual tears. A moan about Colin's job prospects, her going on about having a brandy and me telling her no but other than that –

ZZZZZZZZOOOOOOOOOMMMM!

'*Fuck* – !' I nearly threw myself to the floor and the jolt of movement woke her up, eyes flickering. 'Cathy? Is that… was that, was it thunder or something…? And were you…were you *swearing?*'

'No, no Mum, you're fine, we're fine, it's nothing. One of those-' and I censored myself '-one of those *tubes*. See? This is what I was talking about. About us moving to a lower flat, because that way like the occupational therapist was saying, you'd be able to get out more easily plus we wouldn't have these flying *numpties* -' but she wasn't listening. Tutting, working her head against the pillow, getting comfy, eyes closing against my rant. A minute or so later she was snoring softly again.

I was right though. It *was* dangerous up there, not just because she could have a fall going down the stairs. There'd been an article in *The Scotsman* about police helicopters getting fitted with breathalysers, superheroes having a few drams before they put their capes on. Just because they'd got superpowers, didn't stop them being Scottish. But there was no telling her. She'd get sentimental, going on about the view of the Tay, how elegant the rail bridge was, Tayport misty in the distance. How she and Dad bought this place for the sunsets. Not that Dad was here to see them now. Wherever he was.

Anyway.

I leant over, gave her a kiss goodnight. Not a murmur. Dead to the world and the second I thought the 'd-word', I wished that I hadn't.

I should have got straight to bed knowing the next day at work was going to be hellish in the aftermath of the nonsense outside. But walking past the ladder to the attic, I stopped. Although I didn't want to admit it, didn't want to give those lunatics the satisfaction, part of me wanted to see what was going on. It was like when you're sitting at home and hear fireworks going off somewhere in the city. You *know* they're miles away and you won't see anything but you end up standing at the window, staring at impossible angles, trying to get a view.

What put me off was it was *stupidly* late and up there was my old room. Kept like a shrine up there. As if I'd died. Still, I told myself, I could have a look around, decide what I was going to chuck. I was nearly thirty and there was loads of junk I should have got rid of years ago. I'd been meaning to do it since I moved back but what with Mum and work and everything, I hadn't had the chance. Five, ten minutes, I'd give it.

The Studio I used to call it, pretentious wee git I was, though in my defence I *was* an art student. Used to spend hours up there, Mum passing meals up, nipping down to the toilet when I thought the coast was clear. There was room enough for a small bookcase made by me and Dad out of some planks from a skip, an old-fashioned school desk (the *hassle* we had getting that up there), and a plastic chair that was too big for it. Every other square inch stuffed with piles of comics, and sketchbooks covering the rug I'd made out of squares of carpet taped together from a book of samples Dad had got. The walls covered in pictures, cartoons and comic book covers mostly, some old movie stars – Marlene, Marilyn, Liz Taylor. And yes, it did feel like being stuck inside the head of a fourteen-year-old baby dyke but I surprised myself by liking it. It felt cosy. I could understand why I'd spent so much time up there.

I went to switch the bare bulb on but realised the light of the moon was enough, clear and bright, giving everything a silvery glow. That and the other lights. The weird ones, the supernatural glow of those show-offs. Which is when it clicked. A full moon. *That's* why they were at it, waking up the locals.

Ish had told me about it once in the pub after I'd started winding her up, slagging the Heroes. 'I mean, bridges. What is it with you superhero types and *bridges*. Is it some tourist attraction thing? And why every month? Is it like, hormonal? Like periods or something?'

She hadn't risen to it, hadn't used her powers to blow my eardrums out like any *normal* superhero would have done when dealing with her drunken girlfriend (not ex. Not then). Instead she'd given me this 'You wouldn't understand' look which was only just starting to wind me up. She'd gone to speak then shrugged. 'I don't know. None of us know. It's stronger in some than in others and it just sort of…happens. Y'know?' I nodded, even though of *course* I didn't know, what with me being Normal. 'Whenever there's a full moon we feel the pull. It's like…pigeons.'

'Pigeons? What…like, *were*pigeons?' I snorted and we laughed, the tension easing.

'Yeah, OK, maybe that's a bad example but you know how no one's sure how pigeons find their way when they're flying…' and it was my turn to give her a look. 'So I'm not explaining it very well but it's -'

'Big bloody pigeons,' I'd said, taking a gulp of my pint. '*Dangerous* pigeons with laser eyes and killer breath,' and that was the tension back again. Well done me. Like some toxic superpower. The gift of ruining a decent evening.

Ish. It had been a while since I'd seen her and I wondered if she was out there. I listened carefully, tried to make out from the warped 'Whumphs' and 'Krraaackkks' if there was singing going on. Ish's song, the Silver Selkie letting rip.

Not that I was fussed if she was there or not. None of my business what she got up to. If she wanted to hang about with a load of guys in dodgy spandex under bridges, that was up to her. Got her new friends to play with.

A dark blue light started to fill the room like water rising up past the window and I knew what that meant, who'd arrived to join the party. I craned my neck to see the moon turn blue with the white Saltire across it. What was *really* annoying was my heart started beating faster, letting me know I was as much a sucker for celebrity as anyone else.

The Fantoosh, the Phantom Fantoosh, greatest Scotsman ever born, out there strutting his stuff. Imagine a cross between a young Sean Connery and a Billy Connolly who can fly and lift really heavy stuff. Expressing so much charisma one flash of a smile would see a thousand Grannies swoon.

Flash git.

I was determined not to look, not turn into another fan-girl. I sat down at my desk instead, flicked through the notebook lying on top until I came to the drawing.

A man, a superhero with kiss-curl in place, cape flapping about behind him, one arm stretched out in front of him to help ease him through the air, the skyscrapers surrounding him, 'CAPTAIN FANTASTIC!' in careful capitals arching above him. And I wondered if I realised the resemblance at the time. How much he looked like my Dad.

I must have been, what, fifteen when I drew it? Thinking I had a whole dazzling career as a comic book artist stretching ahead of me. Hah. What if I'd known the truth, what was going to happen ten years later? That when the great leap forward in humanity took place on my front doorstep, superheroes sprouting everywhere, I'd be working as a bloody civil servant, clearing up the mess. Probably chucked myself out of the attic window.

I traced a finger round Captain Fantastic's jawline, trying to keep the bitterness at bay. Maybe I knew back then what was going to happen to Dad and this was me trying to keep a hold of him. Something to remember him by, before he disappeared.

No. Didn't disappear. Was taken. By Kannyman, that mad *bastard* or superbeing or multidimensional whatever-the-fuck they are, who'd taken my Dad along with twenty-nine other Scots. Shortly after that came the Change, Superheroes popping up all over the place, then the folk with Abilities and *Christ*, I wanted my Dad back. Everything back to normal because normal was *good*.

I slammed the book shut, told myself it was the dust causing my eyes to prickle. I tapped the top of the desk then remembered what might be hidden there. Creaked up the lid and…result! Still there, left from the last time I was up, was a half-empty packet of Marlboros and a quarter bottle of vodka, so cheap the label read only 'Vodka'.

'Faaan*tastic!*' and I looked up out the window to see the Fantoosh surrounded by his blue and white shimmery glow flying low along the top of the Rail Bridge. As he passed a shower of glittering purple sparks fell from him, lighting the length of the bridge, the colour of thistles and heather falling into the river.

Naturally because the Fantoosh took this whole being Scottish business *very* seriously. His sponsors would be disappointed if he didn't get his colour-scheme right.

I hated to admit it but it *did* look impressive. Breath-taking even. Put those poncy Edinburgh Festival Fireworks to shame. Aye, bonny Dundee, yah bas!

I pulled open the window and moved the desk back to sit on it while leaning on the window sill. The fag was dry, crackled when I lit it, wouldn't last two minutes but it had been such a long night, the hit of it was bloody *wonderful*.

I took a swig of the vodka, gasping as I gulped. A few years back there'd have been crowds gathering to watch a spectacle like this, the police involved, keeping people back. Now it was random insomniacs like me and some die-hard fans braving the cold to stand by the side of the Tay, cheering on their favourite, hoping for a photo or an autograph.

I did feel some of it that night though. The old magic, when the Change was starting to happen, miracles reported every half hour. I got a shiver up my spine and it wasn't just from the cold. Maybe it was the nicotine, maybe the vodka, but the sweep of the bridge, that massive blue moon electrifying everything, giving the water a satiny look…it got to me. And I felt like that fourteen year old again, in thrall to superpowers.

There were figures caped and in skin-tight suits swooping and dancing around the bridge's struts, playing chicken with a train (there'd be complaints about that), strange electrical charges causing the rails to glow orange, concrete seeming to bend and flow, twisting out into curling decorations. Mini typhoons burst up from the water, dark coloured rainbows rose and vanished. That'd be the Northern Lights, the Cauld Blast causing the blizzard blanking some of the bridge from view, while the blazing horse, the Kelpie, with its flaming mane rode the waves under it, over to Tayport with that idiot, the Golden Eagle swooping down too close, nearly getting his wings singed, feathers skimming the surface of the water to cool them.

And all the while, looping the loop above them, the Phantom Fantoosh was leaving a trail of blue and white behind him, making Paisley patterns in the air, and his turns were so graceful, it was hypnotic watching and I forgot how sometimes on the TV he could come across as a bit of a sleazy chancer, with his day-old stubble and his floppy quiff. Here, he was like some kind of King.

I was starting to get it. Starting to get the point of the whole Flighting business. Since the Change, the *first* Change when the superheroes appeared, most of them have gone corporate. Turned up to open supermarkets, endorsing healthy eating campaigns, promoting Scottish tourism. Well, wasn't as if the country was overrun with supervillains, was it? Here they were enjoying the chance to let their hair down. Let rip. The equivalent of the rest of us, the Normals, getting wasted on a Friday night. I was almost feeling sympathetic, a wee tear in my eye as the fireballs and snowballs and – what was that? ectoplasm? – flew about when I heard it.

No, not it. Ish.

Her song started as a drone, so low I wasn't sure if it was there or not, had to tilt my head to catch it. Then it snagged my ear and poured in, filling me up with an ache, a sweet, sad tone calling me, seeping into my soul, making it thrum and I knew I didn't deserve to hear it, it was too beautiful, too much. Like Liz Fraser and Jeff Buckley and Billie Holiday and Billy MacKenzie combined, too good and pure for the likes of me.

It was Ish but not *my* Ish. Not any more. She'd become the Silver Selkie and she'd set the bridge singing, ringing out in perfect pitch, turning it into one giant instrument. Some of the music was like a celebration but some of it was full of sadness too. It was like she was saying, singing out full-throated, 'Hey! You! All you miserable normal folk, come and look! Isn't this *amazing*! Isn't it *incredible*! And it's awful and *cruel* that you can only watch and we get to *do* this stuff! And how, can somebody please tell me *why*, did everything get so beautifully, so wonderfully, so very fucked up!'

I listened a few minutes more until I'd had enough, couldn't bear it and slammed the window shut against the chill and Ish's song. Listened instead for my Mum crying in the dark.

Chapter 2
Busy day for Benefits – the fearsome Slorach – a troublesome client

The drive in to the Benefits Agency the next day wasn't as bad as I'd expected. Usually after a Flighting it was a nightmare, what with stray laser blasts having knocked down trees or some joker giving traffic lights independent thought so they ended up having these existentialist debates with pedestrians, 'Yes, but *why* do you want to cross to the other side?' But apart from a lump of blue smouldering something I had to swerve around on the Lochee Road, it was fine.

After such a display by the big Boys and Girls, the folk with Abilities would get ratty, demand their claim get passed through faster, complain about all the attention being paid to Heroes. When I swung Martina, my Mitsubishi Colt, into the Agency's car park it wasn't too busy and that seemed a good sign. Should have known better. A pair of bastard Knoxians were there at the door, handing out their leaflets of doom, telling folk with Abilities that if they only changed their ways, gave up drinking, drugs, everything that made life better, they'd be cured. I glared at them as I walked past and they nodded, soor-faced at me, giving me a quick blast of guilt to which I replied with a satisfying 'Fuck off'. Stepping into the foyer, the waiting area for clients before they meet their case officer, I had to resist the urge to turn and walk right back past them. Bloody Heroes.

A few months after the Change and the initial wave of proper, bona fide Superheroes, with back stories and origin myths and everything, those with Abilities started appearing. And when they began claiming benefits, a few incidents took place at the office, people with *dis*abilities getting narked at the freaks jumping the queue. So the area was split, a three-inch-thick Perspex floor-to-ceiling screen dividing it, stopping a few feet before the Reception desk. It was supposed to offer protection but was so scarred and dented, pockmarked with burn holes, that it made you feel *less* safe seeing it.

The side you entered was where the Normal folk sat, waiting to complain about how long their Disability Living Allowance was taking to come through or asking why their Working Tax Credits had been cut. There were only a handful there that day and the way they were gawping at what was going on one the other side of the screen made me strongly suspect they'd only come in because This Morning wasn't on for some reason.

Because the other side was *mobbed*, absolute mayhem. The front row of plastic seating was taken up by a group of women who all looked similar. At first I thought they were sisters but then the one in the middle looked more *solid* than the others on either side of her, who were blurred round the edges, and I realised those weren't her sisters, they were fainter copies of her. Then there was this older guy who looked shattered, dancing about the place like a crap version of Riverdance shouting, 'Can't, can't stay still! If I do, I'll sink, sink into the floor!' A young guy was leaning against the Perspex, bare palm flat against it, melting it, pushing the material out slowly, like a Hollywood superstar leaving his mark outside the Chinese Theatre.

I tapped the Perspex next to his head, pointing out the damage he was doing. He gave me a 'What you gonna do about it?' stare that I returned with interest having spent five years dealing with arsey clients like him, one that said 'I may be short but I don't take no shit.' Slowly he lowered his hand, pretended to take an interest in the woman in the row next to him whose hair had been replaced by a halo of flickering blue flames like a human pilot light. I knew, I just *knew* from the smile spreading across his face he was thinking of lighting a fag off her. Because I was thinking exactly the same thing.

The mild hangover I thought I'd managed to avoid after downing the rest of that vodka threatened to make an appearance when I walked into the office and got hit by a wave of caseworker chatter. The Special Abilities Claimant Section (or SACS as it was referred to with a snigger) was housed in a large open plan office with subbies of four dotted about the place. Practically every one of the fifty-odd caseworkers had their headsets on, talking to clients. Instead of processing claims they'd be explaining why it was taking so long (mainly because the idiots kept calling us up).

I was about to sneak off to the vending machine for a much needed coffee when a voice chillier than a kiss from the Cauld Blast froze me to the spot.

'So nice of you to join us, Cathy.'

I swivelled carefully in part because of my headache but mainly because it was always wise to prepare yourself before facing off with the Slorach. That was Mrs Sheena Slorach, Section Leader of SACS, sitting behind the desk at the head of the room that gave her a commanding view of everyone, a one-woman Panopticon. The only way you're ever likely to meet a woman more terrifying is if Margaret Thatcher rose from the grave, zombified. In her late fifties she had an embalmed quality, hair so fixed and immovable it looked more like some wood-effect plastic. Her make-up was applied mask-thick and sometimes I'd wake up at 3am from a dream where it had slipped off, revealing the lizard creature beneath.

There was definitely something lizard-like about her eyes that morning. She'd never liked me with my jeans and my t-shirts and my never wearing my stupid bloody security pass. I'd kept a blue streak in my black hair which I hated for weeks just to piss her off.

'Sheena, look, it's only half nine, I'm not staggering in at 11 and anyway, I'm down for a late -'

'I've forwarded some emails to you,' she near whispered and I'm sure the noise from the surrounding subbies died down a little. Nosey bastards. 'They'd been sent into the general team inbox but due to their...' the Slorach gave a light cough, '*nature* and the fact he was one of your clients, I've forwarded them to you. After you read them you may want to…' She picked up a red felt tip pen and clutched it hard, as though it was an organ of the client in question, '…you may want to pay them a visit. Don't worry about losing time. I'll put an update through for you. Official business.'

There was a gasp from a subby and I clutched the corner of the Slorach's desk. The Slorach was Old School, didn't have much truck with that whole 'client is always right' shite. She saw clients less as suffering individuals than awkward buggers who got in the way of us doing our job. She also hated letting caseworkers out of her sight because she assumed that instead of doing a full assessment we'd be off home catching up on *Four in a Bed*. Which was *completely* lacking in trust and *entirely* accurate. So for her to suggest not only I go see a client in need but that she'd give me time for it was enough to make me wonder if Kannyman had been up to their old tricks, messing with the laws of the universe.

'Ehmm…right, OK, I'll…I'll…there were those other cases you were wanting me to have a look at, the ones that had to get sorted by the end of this week? I've got most of them—'

'They can be put on hold,' and the Slorach snapped off the top of her pen with a sound like bone cracking. 'I'll pass them to another officer to deal with. I want you to give full priority to those emails. Once you've read them I'm sure you'll understand my concern. And I know I don't have to tell you this, Cathy, but I would very much appreciate your discretion on this matter. Email me your findings.'

'What was all *that* about?' Becky whispered as soon as I'd sat down at my subby, peering through the gap between our computers. Becky had only been at SACS for two years, one of the new batch brought in when the bosses finally admitted the Benefits system was crumbling under the demand of the Abled. She was in her early twenties, not as cynical and worn-out as her colleagues which meant she came across either as refreshingly perky or bloody irritating. She was wearing *pigtails* that morning and I winced at her interest.

Jamie sat next to her, the same age, fresh out of the Art School. On his first day here he'd laughed when I'd told him I'd been there. Still not entirely sure how I'd managed to not kill him. He had the hipster, or 'twat' look as I preferred to call it and of *course* he was in a band, seemed to use SACS as a place to get some sleep in between rehearsals. He was giving the autopilot spiel about which forms the client would need to download but even though he'd got the croaky voice and black-baggy eyes of a late night aftermath, he was staring at me, obviously keen for any distraction from the phones.

'I'd love to tell you, honest I would, Becky,' I sucked my teeth as I switched my computer on, 'but then I'd have to kill you.'

'Go on, tell her, *pleeeease!*' Jamie begged and I was hoping he'd hung up on that client as I wagged a finger at him.

'Jamie, we've had this conversation. Promoting the murder of your colleagues is something we do not do in this team. We're short-staffed as it is.'

Becky slapped the top of his arm and he gave a wee cry, clutched it, looking at me in appeal, 'Oh, right, so no killing but other forms of physical violence are alright, are they?'

'Jamie,' I could hear the electronic chirrup of a call coming through his computer, 'haven't you a client to answer?' He scowled, saluting with his middle finger when Becky said 'Hope it's Mr Gilbert again.' Mr Gilbert was one of the Names, a select group who'd gained infamy within SACS for being complete fucking arseholes. Gilbert's supposed Ability was compulsive word-play, conversations involving puns, one-liners, limericks and long explanations for the origins of such phrases as 'a hiding to nothing.' He'd been consistently refused a full assessment as his Ability, according to the guidelines, did 'not pose a threat to the client's or to the public's safety.' Which was ironic considering after five minutes of his nonsense you either wanted to throttle him or strangle yourself with your headset cord.

'Now, now children, remember, respect in the workplace,' I reminded them but I was glad of the banter, taking my mind off whatever was waiting for me in my inbox and Becky wouldn't be stopped. 'The Slorach doesn't usually speak to *anyone* of a morning. Alan thought maybe you were getting your P45.'

'Aw gee Alan, thanks for your support,' I teased as Alan next to me gave a soft chuckle. A middle-aged experienced caseworker who displayed, much to HR's continuing frustration, absolutely no desire to climb the career ladder, he'd been happy to stay in the same grade for the past fifteen years. Which meant he was one of the few left who knew his stuff, had trained me up when I joined all those years ago. He looked dull – grey hair, serial killer glasses, tie and one of those shirts chequered with the blue boxes you find in Maths exercise books – and he could be, especially when he was going on about football. But underneath that there was a sly humour, a fine knowledge of sixties and seventies pop and a talent for acoustic guitar as displayed occasionally at the SACS Christmas party.

After clicking onto Outlook, I saw the email address and subject headings of the emails the Slorach had forwarded and groaned, put my head in my hands as Alan asked 'Fun Monday is it?' Muttering, 'Davey Robertson. Bloody Davey Robertson. You will be the death of me,' I almost, *almost* marched up to the Slorach and demanded to be put on the phones, as discussing with Mr Gilbert the origin of 'arguing the toss' would be preferable to the mess awaiting me.

The story continues …

Kirsti Wishart is an Edinburgh-based writer of short stories, novels and other things. Her stories have appeared in *New Writing Scotland, 404 Ink, Glasgow Review of Books, Product Magazine* and been shortlisted for the Scottish Arts Trust Story Awards. She's been a Hawthornden Fellow, a contestant in Literary Death Match and is a regular contributor to *The One O'Clock Gun*, a literary free-sheet found mostly in Edinburgh pubs.

Her debut novel, The Knitting Station, was published by Rymour Books in 2021 with her second, The Projectionist, selected by SNACK magazine as one of the ten best Scottish books of 2022.

The Pocketbook Guide to
Scottish Superheroes
– Kirsty Wishart

When we invited Kirsty to send us a story for SF Caledonia she also asked if we were interested in a novel she had written. It's about an alternative Scotland where folk randomly develop superpowers, she said.

We're not really geared up for publishing full length works, but if you're willing to experiment, how about releasing it as an online serial on SF Caledonia?

Kirsti agreed, tweaked it a little to accommodate the format, and here are the first two chapters.

If you have enjoyed the story so far you can continue online, using the link below.

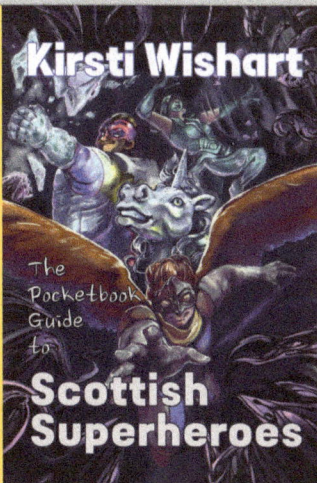

Kirsti Wishart

The Pocketbook Guide to **Scottish Superheroes**

The story continues ..
sfcaledonia.scot/urls/ssh

Space

John Buchan

L eithen told me this story one evening in early September as we sat beside the pony track which gropes its way from Glenvalin up the Correi na Sidhe. I had arrived that afternoon from the south, while he had been taking an off-day from a week's stalking, so we had walked up the glen together after tea to get the news of the forest. A rifle was out on the Correi na Sidhe beat, and a thin spire of smoke had risen from the top of Sgurr Dearg to show that a stag had been killed at the burnhead. The lumpish hill pony with its deer-saddle had gone up the Correi in a gillie's charge while we followed at leisure, picking our way among the loose granite rocks and the patches of wet bogland. The track climbed high on one of the ridges of Sgurr Dearg, till it hung over a caldron of green glen with the Alt-na-Sidhe churning in its linn a thousand feet below. It was a breathless evening, I remember, with a pale-blue sky just clearing from the haze of the day. West-wind weather may make the North, even in September, no bad imitation of the Tropics, and I sincerely pitied the man who all these stifling hours had been toiling on the screes of Sgurr Dearg. By-and-by we sat down on a bank of heather, and idly watched the trough swimming at our feet. The clatter of the pony's hoofs grew fainter, the drone of bees had gone, even the midges seemed to have forgotten their calling. No place on earth can be so deathly still as a deer-forest early in the season before the stags have begun roaring, for there are no sheep with their homely noises, and only the rare croak of a raven breaks the silence. The hillside was far from sheer-one could have walked down with a little care-but something in the shape of the hollow and the remote gleam of white water gave it an extraordinary depth and space. There was a shimmer left from the day's heat, which invested bracken and rock and scree with a curious airy unreality. One could almost have believed that the eye had tricked the mind, that all was mirage, that five yards from the path the solid earth fell away into nothingness. I have a bad head, and instinctively I drew farther back into the heather. Leithen's eyes were looking vacantly before him.

"Did you ever know Hollond?" he asked.

Then he laughed shortly. "I don't know why I asked that, but somehow this place reminded me of Hollond. That glimmering hollow looks as if it were the beginning of eternity. It must be eerie to live with the feeling always on one."

Leithen seemed disinclined for further exercise. He lit a pipe and smoked quietly for a little. "Odd that you didn't know Hollond. You must have heard his name. I thought you amused yourself with metaphysics."

Then I remembered. There had been an erratic genius who had written some articles in Mind on that dreary subject, the mathematical conception of infinity. Men had praised them to me, but I confess I never quite understood their argument. "Wasn't he some sort of mathematical professor?" I asked.

"He was, and, in his own way, a tremendous swell. He wrote a book on Number which has translations in every European language. He is dead now, and the Royal Society founded a medal in his honour. But I wasn't thinking of that side of him."

It was the time and place for a story, for the pony would not be back for an hour. So I asked Leithen about the other side of Hollond which was recalled to him by Correi na Sidhe. He seemed a little unwilling to speak...

"I wonder if you will understand it. You ought to, of course, better than me, for you know something of philosophy. But it took me a long time to get the hang of it, and I can't give you any kind of explanation. He was my fag at Eton, and when I began to get on at the Bar I was able to advise him on one or two private matters, so that he rather fancied my legal ability. He came to me with his story because he had to tell someone, and he wouldn't trust a colleague. He said he didn't want a scientist to know, for scientists were either pledged to their own theories and wouldn't understand, or, if they understood, would get ahead of him in his researches. He wanted a lawyer, he said, who was accustomed to weighing evidence. That was good sense, for evidence must always be judged by the same laws, and I suppose in the long-run the most abstruse business comes down to a fairly simple deduction from certain data. Anyhow, that was the way he used to talk, and I listened to him, for I liked the man, and had an enormous respect for his brains. At Eton he sluiced down all the mathematics they could give him, and he was an astonishing swell at Cambridge. He was a simple fellow, too, and talked no more jargon than he could help. I used to climb with him in the Alps now and then, and you would never have guessed that he had any thoughts beyond getting up steep rocks.

"It was at Chamonix, I remember, that I first got a hint of the matter that was filling his mind. We had been taking an off-day, and were sitting in the hotel garden, watching the Aiguilles getting purple in the twilight. Chamonix always makes me choke a little-it is so crushed in by those great snow masses. I said something about it—said I liked the open spaces like the Gornegrat or the Bel Alp better. He asked me why: if it was the difference of the air, or merely the wider horizon? I said it was the sense of not being crowded, of living in an empty world. He repeated the word 'empty' and laughed.

"'By "empty" you mean,' he said, 'where things don't knock up against you?'

I told him No. I mean just empty, void, nothing but blank aether.

"You don't knock up against things here, and the air is as good as you want. It can't be the lack of ordinary emptiness you feel."

"I agreed that the word needed explaining. 'I suppose it is mental restlessness,' I said. 'I like to feel that for a tremendous distance there is nothing round me. Why, I don't know. Some men are built the other way and have a terror of space.'

"He said that that was better. 'It is a personal fancy, and depends on your KNOWING that there is nothing between you and the top of the Dent Blanche. And you know because your eyes tell you there is nothing. Even if you were blind, you might have a sort of sense about adjacent matter. Blind men often have it. But in any case, whether got from instinct or sight, the KNOWLEDGE is what matters.'

"Hollond was embarking on a Socratic dialogue in which I could see little point. I told him so, and he laughed. "'I am not sure that I am very clear myself. But yes—there IS a point. Supposing you knew-not by sight or by instinct, but by sheer intellectual knowledge, as I know the truth of a mathematical proposition— that what we call empty space was full, crammed. Not with lumps of what we call matter like hills and houses, but with things as real—as real to the mind. Would you still feel crowded?'

"'No,' I said, 'I don't think so. It is only what we call matter that signifies. It would be just as well not to feel crowded by the other thing, for there would be no escape from it. But what are you getting at? Do you mean atoms or electric currents or what?'

"He said he wasn't thinking about that sort of thing, and began to talk of another subject.

"Next night, when we were pigging it at the Geant cabane, he started again on the same tack. He asked me how I accounted for the fact that animals could find their way back over great tracts of unknown country. I said I supposed it was the homing instinct.

"'Rubbish, man,' he said. 'That's only another name for the puzzle, not an explanation. There must be some reason for it. They must KNOW something that we cannot understand. Tie a cat in a bag and take it fifty miles by train and it will make its way home. That cat has some clue that we haven't.'

"I was tired and sleepy, and told him that I did not care a rush about the psychology of cats. But he was not to be snubbed, and went on talking.

"'How if Space is really full of things we cannot see and as yet do not know? How if all animals and some savages have a cell in their brain or a nerve which responds to the invisible world? How if all Space be full of these landmarks, not material in our sense, but quite real? A dog barks at nothing, a wild beast makes an aimless circuit. Why? Perhaps because Space is made up of corridors and alleys, ways to travel and things to shun? For all we know, to a greater intelligence than ours the top of Mont Blanc may be as crowded as Piccadilly Circus.'

"But at that point I fell asleep and left Hollond to repeat his questions to a guide who knew no English and a snoring porter.

. . .

The story continues at
www.sfcaledonia.scot/space-by-john-buchan/

where you can also watch Jonathan Whiteside reading
Space

Space was published in *The Moon Endureth—Tales and Fancies*, published in 1912.

This version of the story was taken from Project Gutenberg.

SF Caledonia — more free reading

Welcome to the last page, but don't stop now. Here are a couple more tasty treats for you to enjoy on SF Caledonia...

The Honey Trap
Ruth EJ Booth

"What the hell is that?"

The apple looked awful. A piebald runt in red and yellow-green, with a sandpaper roughness around its bear-stub stalk. A bulge threatened one side of its thick-looking matte skin, squeezing creases into its squat sides. It sat on the table like an insult, a gnarled middle finger to the perfected #04B404 Foods Agency standard that reigned the international markets.

Jack Becker – accredited independent collective operator, award-winning Growth Guru, author, cult TV personality – plucked up the fruit in one rubber-gloved hand.

"I have never," he said, "ever seen such a hideous-looking apple before. Truly."

Secret Ingredients
Callum McSorley

I'm a line cook. This is how I became a spy:

I come from a binary solar system. We don't have what other beings might call day and night. Nor do we measure days like they measure days, or years like they measure years. I can't tell you how old I am, not in a way that would satisfy you. All I can say is, the first time I saw the dark – the real, deep dark – was the first time I left home. I looked out at the obsidian void from the window of the ship, and knew I was gone and never going back. Goodbye, Mama. Goodbye, Papa.

www.sfcaledonia.scot

www.ingramcontent.com/pod-product-compliance
Ingram Content Group UK Ltd.
Pitfield, Milton Keynes, MK11 3LW, UK
UKHW050156140325
456222UK00012B/27

9 781739 535933